Caught Between a Rock
and a Soft Place!

"You with the gun!" he shouted, his voice carrying above the babble of excited voices. "Drop the pistol and turn around with your hands over your head!"

For a moment it had seemed that the running man was going to obey, for he hesitated, stopped and began swivelling around in response to Longarm's command. Halfway through his turn, he grabbed the arm of the nearest of the fleeing girls and pulled her to him, using her as a shield.

He had brought up his gun as he moved, and Longarm was looking down its muzzle.

"Don't do nothing foolish!" the gun-wielder called. He swung the muzzle of the weapon to threaten the people who were now pressing against the wall or crouching under tables...

TABOR EVANS

LONGARM

IN THE TEXAS PANHANDLE

A JOVE BOOK

LONGARM IN THE TEXAS PANHANDLE

A Jove Book/published by arrangement with
Context, Inc.

PRINTING HISTORY
Jove edition/March 1986

ISBN: 0-515-08495-6

Chapter 1

Through the bluish haze of smoke from his long, thin cheroot, Longarm studied the face of the young woman sitting beside him in the window seat of the Union Pacific Railroad passenger coach. Her head was half-turned from him as she gazed at the lovely spectacle of the Rocky Mountain sunrise.

"It's right pretty, ain't it, Alila?" Longarm asked.

"Oh, yes," the girl agreed. "The little mountains back East aren't more than humps compared to these."

As Alila turned back to look out the window, a half-smile twitched Longarm's lips under his longhorn moustache as the thought popped into his mind that, unlike most of the women he'd escorted into Denver on a train, his companion on this trip wasn't wearing handcuffs. In fact, she was a cut above most of the women he'd run into at any of the places like Bill Tucker's Cowboy's Rest saloon in Ogallala.

For one thing, Alila was younger than most saloon girls. She couldn't be much more than in her early twenties. She wasn't dressed like a saloon girl, either. Alila wore a dark

1

blue serge dress, which emphasized the gold of her hair that looped in a gentle wave over her ears below the narrow, upcurled brim of her low-crowned travelling hat. Her eyes picked up the blue of the dress and gave them the hue of violets. Her lips were full but firm, and her high cheekbones bore no touch of rouge, but glowed pink under the thinnest possible film of powder.

"How much farther is it to Denver?" she asked.

"Not far," Longarm replied. "We'll be pulling into the depot in about another hour."

"What's Denver like, Marshal Long?"

"Oh, it's a nice enough town, Alila. Far's I'm concerned, it's just a bedroom, because most of the time I'm off someplace else, working on a case."

"No, I mean, what's it really like?" Alila persisted. "You've got to know more about it than I do. This is the first time I've ever been to Denver, or anyplace else out West here. I hope it isn't like Ogallala, because—" She stopped suddenly and turned her face away, back toward the window.

Longarm said nothing. He understood the reason for her reaction.

After a moment, without turning her head, Alila went on in a low voice, "I just want to forget all about Ogallala and the Cowboy's Rest."

"Can't say I blame you for that, Alila," Longarm nodded. "You had a pretty rough time of it there."

"I think I'd just like to look out the window and not talk any more for a minute or two, Marshal Long. Would you mind?"

"Not a bit," Longarm replied promptly. Alila's voice had been very sober, and he knew that she was recalling what had happened last night at the Cowboy's Rest.

Longarm hadn't planned to go to Ogallala himself. It had become his destination because of an unexpected twist in a case that had started three weeks earlier in Steamboat Springs. Billy Vail had sent Longarm to the Springs from Denver because he was the only free deputy the office had,

2

and Longarm had expected to bring his case to a quick conclusion.

Instead, he had spent three full weeks on the trail of a bandit who had murdered the postmaster in Steamboat Springs during a robbery. Longarm had arrived at the Springs two days after the bandit eluded the Routt County sheriff. Then he had spent another day scouting, trying to find the killer's trail.

The trail led him into the rugged foothills of the Great Divide, southeast to Rabbit Ears Pass, and then a hundred miles across the rolling flats to Steamboat Pass. On the east side of the second pass, the fleeing outlaw had angled to the north, across the high prairie country at the southeastern corner of Wyoming and almost a hundred miles farther, into the rolling Nebraska prairieland.

On the comparatively level prairie, Longarm had finally managed to overcome the fleeing outlaw's three-day lead. He had caught up with his quarry on the north bank of the Platte, where the fugitive murderer had put himself into a corner at the point where Otter Creek flowed into the river. Trapped on a spit of land at the juncture of the two streams, the killer had chosen to shoot it out with Longarm, and hadn't lived to face a hangman's noose.

Since the livery horse he had rented in Steamboat Springs was in even worse condition than Longarm was, the deputy took stock of his situation after burying the fugitive's body. The horse had a lame fetlock, and Longarm was not foolish enough to try to retrace his trail on the back of a crippled and exhausted mount. The nearest settlement of any size was the booming town of Ogallala, on the Union Pacific main line. That simplified shipping his exhausted horse back to Steamboat Springs and allowed Longarm to ride back to Denver in the comfortable seat of a passenger coach.

When he rode into Ogallala after two more long days in the saddle, Longarm hadn't had any idea that he would be escorting a pretty young dance-hall girl when he left the town. At that time, all he had been interested in was getting a night or two of uninterrupted sleep in a reasonably comfortable bed, and the Cowboy's Rest was a combination saloon and hotel that fit his requirements. Even if Bill Tucker, the establishment's owner and manager, hadn't been a friend of long standing, Longarm still would have headed there.

Just as he had anticipated, most of Longarm's weariness vanished after a good meal and a hot bath in the big wooden tub down the hall from his room. He began to feel like his old self when he woke from a night of sound sleep. Hot meals in the Cowboy's Rest dining room instead of a few hurried bites of jerky and parched corn eaten in the saddle also helped with Longarm's quick return to normality, and so did a reasonable number of drinks of Tom Moore Maryland rye at the saloon.

By the end of his second day at the Cowboy's Rest, Longarm was ready to start back to Denver. He went into the combination saloon and dance hall that was one of the establishment's biggest drawing cards. As he had expected, he found Bill Tucker sitting at a small table in the back of the room.

Tucker was sipping a glass of seltzer water. The tinkling of a honkytonk tune from the piano made speech at a distance impossible. When Tucker saw Longarm, the saloon owner raised his hand and gave a signal to the barkeep, then pointed to Longarm. By the time Longarm had threaded his way through the dozen or so roughly dressed cowhands who were dancing with the saloon girls and reached Tucker's table, the barkeep was placing a bottle of Tom Moore and a glass on the table.

Settling into the chair across the table from the owner, Longarm poured himself a drink of the Maryland rye. He raised his glass in a silent salute to Tucker and let the pungent whiskey trickle down his throat before lighting one of his long, thin cheroots.

"Looks like I'll be leaving you in the morning, Bill," Longarm told his old friend. "And I sure don't figure you're going to be getting up to see me off at the depot at three o'clock in the morning."

"You're right about that." Tucker smiled. "I'm usually just thinking about going to bed at that time of day."

"I sort of hate to go," Longarm went on, refilling his glass and taking another puff on his cigar. "You run a real nice place here, Bill."

Tucker nodded. "Thanks, Longarm." Then he went on, "I didn't expect you to stay as long as you have. Whenever you stop by you're generally in and out in a couple of hours."

"Well, I figured I had a little bit of rest coming, after I saved the government the expense of a trial and a hanging. But if I don't report back to Billy Vail by the day after tomorrow, he's going to have a lot to say about me wasting time when we're so shorthanded at the office."

"Be sure to remember me to Billy," Tucker said. "Tell him I'll be real mad at him if he doesn't stop in the next time he can unglue his butt from that swivel chair in his office and ride up this way."

"I'll do that." Longarm placed his glass on the table and stood up. Extending his hand to Tucker, he went on, "I'll settle up my account before I go to bed. Then I can sleep a few minutes longer in the morning."

"You'll settle up nothing," Tucker told him. "How many times do I have to tell you that as long as I'm running the Cowboy's Rest your money's no good here?"

"It don't come outa my pocket," Longarm protested. "I just put it on my expense voucher, and the government pays me back."

"Then let's just say I figure I owe the government something for giving us a free country where a man can start from nowhere and make a good place for himself," Tucker replied. "I might not be getting rich, but as long as the government stays out of my way I can get along all right."

"You're the boss," Longarm replied. I'd like to see—"

A shot from the dance floor cut him off. He whipped his Colt from its cross-draw holster as he swivelled to face the dancers.

A man's limp form sprawling facedown in the middle of the dance floor drew Longarm's attention away from the couples scattering toward the sides of the big barnlike room. As Longarm's eyes flicked over the scene, he saw that one of the men running toward the wall had a revolver in his hand. Without knowing what had caused the shooting, Longarm could not justify cutting down the man carrying the pistol without first challenging him.

"You with the gun!" he shouted, his voice carrying above the babble of excited voices. "Drop the pistol and turn around with your hands up over your head!"

For a moment it had seemed that the running man was going to obey, for he hesitated, stopped, and began swivelling around in response to Longarm's command. Halfway through his turn, he grabbed the arm of the nearest of the fleeing girls and pulled her to him. When he completed his turn, his arm was around the girl, clutching her to him, using her as a shield. He had brought up his gun as he moved, and Longarm was looking down its muzzle.

"Don't do nothing foolish!" the gun-wielder called. He swung the muzzle of the weapon to threaten the people who were now pressing against the wall or crouching under tables. "And you can just drop that Colt of yours, Long! I damn sure don't aim to let you take me back!"

Because the head of the girl the gunman had grabbed obscured his face, Longarm had not been able to identify him. Now, the rough voice rang a bell, and he could put a name to the gunman.

Raising his own voice, Longarm said, "You ain't got a chance, Blackie! All them men around you and behind you have got guns, and the minute you pull the trigger they'll cut you down."

"Not as long as I got this pretty young lady, they won't," Blackie replied. "They ain't about to take a chance of killing her."

Longarm replied confidently, "You can't get away, Blackie. If you've got any sense, you'll give up peaceful. Now, toss that gun on the floor before the lady twists away from you, because the minute she does, I'll shoot."

Although Longarm didn't have a great deal of hope that the dance-hall girl would take his hint, she'd surprised him by moving at once. Almost before he's stopped speaking, Blackie's captive suddenly let her muscles go limp, and the dead weight of her sagging body pulled the gunman off balance before he could tighten his grip on her.

As the girl's fall freed her from Blackie's encircling arm, the gunman instinctively bent forward with her. Longarm waited only until he had a clear shot at Blackie's slanting head before he triggered his Colt. The outlaw was pushed back by the impact of Longarm's slug. His dying reflex tightened his forefinger on his pistol's cocked trigger, but the bullet thunked harmlessly into the dance floor.

The cowhands who had been crouching along the walls and under the scanty protection of the tables converged on the two bodies that lay on the floor. Longarm pushed through the milling crowd.

"All right, folks!" Longarm called, raising his voice to be heard above the hubbub. "Clear away, now, and let me see if I can figure out what this was all about."

Tucker's voice cut through the dying chatter. "The bar's closed as of now! So's this room! You girls go to your rooms, and you men clear out."

Slowly the babble subsided as the big room began to empty. By this time Longarm had reached the spot where Blackie's body lay. A few feet away, the dance-hall girl had gotten to her feet and was standing, swaying unsteadily, her eyes wide open, her mouth slack. Longarm had seen enough cases of shock to realize her condition. He took her gently by the arm and led her to the closet chair.

"Don't try to move or stand up," he told her, his voice low but firm. "You just sit still till your nerves get settled. And don't go off with the other girls. I'll need to ask you a few questions when you're fit to talk."

Although she nodded in response to his instructions, Longarm wasn't sure she had really understood them. He watched her for a moment to make sure she would be all right. Then he stepped over to Bill Tucker, who was standing beside Blackie's huddled body.

"From what this fellow said, I got the idea you've run into him before," Tucker said as Longarm stopped beside him.

"Yep, I remember him now, Bill. His name's Lenny Frost, but everyone called him Blackie. For a minute I

7

couldn't place him, because he's dropped off a lot of weight since I taken him in for a mail-car holdup over up by North Platte," Longarm replied. "The judge put him away for ten years, and that was six years ago, so I reckon he must've busted outa the pen."

Tucker nodded thoughtfully. "That'd explain why he was so quick on the trigger, then. I know I've never seen him before tonight, and I don't often miss recognizing a regular customer. The other fellow, the one he killed, I placed him right away. He's a hand on the Half-Moon spread, upriver about eight miles. His friends call him Fred."

"Has he ever been in trouble that you know of?"

"No. But he might've run across the law some time, before he landed at the Half-Moon."

Turning to look at the girl, who still sat quietly in the chair where he had placed her, Longarm said, "Maybe the girl over there can tell us something more, but I figure the fellow just grabbed her because she was the closest one to him when he decided to get away from me."

"Alila hasn't been here long enough to've gotten acquainted with many of my customers." Tucker frowned. "Less than a month, if I remember correctly."

"Her name's sorta funny," Longarm remarked. "But I guess she's like most of the girls that wind up in her kind of job—takes a new name because she's run away from home or something like that."

"That's likely," Tucker agreed. He followed Longarm to the chair where Alila was sitting. "I don't ask 'em to many questions, you know."

They stopped in front of the seated girl. Longarm asked her, "You think you're up to answering a few questions now?"

Alila nodded. "I'm over being scared, if that's what you mean," she said. "But I don't think I'm going to be much help to you, Mr. Long."

"He's a U. S. marshal, Alila," Tucker volunteered. "I've known him quite a while, and you don't need to be a bit afraid of him."

"Well, I know I don't have anything to worry about,"

she replied. "I'd never seen that man the marshal shot until just before the trouble started. He was standing by me at the bar and he struck up a conversation with me. Well, that's what Mr. Tucker pays us girls for, to talk to the customers and dance with them, so I talked to him."

"You hadn't't seen him in here before?" Longarm asked.

Alila shook her head. "No. Of course, that doesn't mean he hasn't been here. I guess Mr. Tucker told you I just started working for him a little while ago."

Longarm nodded, then asked, "You didn't notice anything odd about him?"

"No," the girl said thoughtfully. "He just talked, like all the rest. I could tell he was getting ready to ask me to dance with him when Fred came in and—"

"Hold on," Longarm interrupted. He turned to Tucker. "You said the man Blackie shot was named Fred, didn't you?"

Tucker nodded. "Yes." He walked to the body that lay face-down on the floor and bent to peer at the face. "This is Fred, all right."

"Oh, no!" Alila gasped. "Fred was such a nice man. He was polite and sort of bashful. It just makes me feel sick when I think about that man killing him."

"Now, don't go thinking any of what's happened was your fault," Longarm consoled her. "That Blackie was about half-crazy when I arrested him a few years ago. I guess he got worse after he'd served some time."

"I didn't do a thing to make him mad." Alila frowned. "He didn't have anything to say after Fred came up and I said hello to him. Then Fred said he had to go out and see to his horse if he was going to stay and dance, and he started for the door. The other man, that Blackie, he left, too. Then I heard the shot and I got so scared I don't remember anything else."

"I sorta figured that was the way of it," Longarm said. "And you don't have a thing to worry about. I'll have to put your name in my report when I write it up, but there's not going to be a trial or anything like that."

"Just the same, I don't want to keep on working here,"

she said decisively. "I don't think I'd feel right about it."

"Well, now, that's up to you, Alila," Tucker said. "I won't blame you a bit if you feel like you want to quit."

"I guess I do," Alila replied. "Except I'm sort of scared to go anyplace else all by myself."

"Marshal Long's heading back to Denver in the morning," Tucker told her. "I don't suppose he'd mind it if you took the same train he is, so you'd feel you had company."

Alila turned to Longarm. "Would you mind, Marshal?"

"Not a bit. Except, if you're aiming to catch that train, you'll have to pack in time to be at the depot at three o'clock in the morning. Think you can manage that?"

"Of course I can," she said. "It's not quite midnight now, and I've only got one suitcase to pack."

"Go ahead, then," Tucker told her. "While you're packing, I'll tote up what you've earned and have your money waiting by the time you and Longarm are ready to leave."

For the first hour of their trip, Alila had slept fitfully. When the dawn light began to brighten the landscape and filter into the coach, she had awakened and looked around with a startled expression on her face. Then, as Longarm wished her good morning, she had sighed and settled down. She had said little after her reply to his greeting, but had turned her head to the window.

Longarm had respected her obvious wish to be silent, and they'd exchanged only a few words until she'd asked him to tell her about Denver. Now Longarm sat silently, puffing his cheroot, but before he'd smoked it down to a stub Alila turned back to him.

"I'm sorry," she said. "I didn't mean to be so rude to you, but I just couldn't help it. Now tell me about Denver, Marshal Long."

Chapter 2

Longarm was silent for a moment, trying to decide how to start. Finally he said, "Well, Denver ain't such a bad place, Alila. Except when it snows, that is. And in winter it can get cold as a witch's—" He caught himself, and stopped before finishing his sentence.

Alila said quickly, "You don't have to be afraid you'll shock me, Marshal Long. I guess I've heard all the words you men use when there ain't—I mean, aren't—any ladies around. You were about to say 'cold as a witch's tit,' weren't you?"

"Matter of fact, I was." Longarm grinned a bit sheepishly. "But I sorta remember you and me had made a deal while we was waiting for this train to pull in. You said it sounded real cold and formal for me to call you 'Miss Alila,' and I told you I wouldn't if you'd just call me plain 'Longarm.'"

"I'll sure try, if that's what you want me to do," she agreed. "Now, go on and tell me what Denver's like."

"I guess you'd say it's a cut above most places," Longarm began, frowning thoughtfully. "It ain't like some places I've

11

been where there's a lot of soot and stink in the air. And it ain't a pricey place to live, either. You can get a real nice meal for half a dollar in a pretty good restaurant. They've been building a lot of new houses there lately, so room rent's real reasonable."

"Do you think I can find a job there?"

"Why, a smart, nice-looking girl like you ought not have lot of trouble. The question that comes to my mind is, what're you good at? You must've been working someplace before you left home and wound up at the Cowboy's Rest."

"My last job was in a millinery shop," she replied. "And before that I worked for a dressmaker. I never did work in a place like Mr. Tucker's before, but that was the only job I could find in Ogallala. And I can do housework, of course."

"You oughta find a job pretty quick, then. There's a passel of rich folks in Denver that hires maids. And there's plenty of shops where they make ladies' hats to sell, and two or three good-sized department stores."

Alila sighed with relief. "That makes me feel better," she said. "I guess I'll manage all right."

"Sure you will," Longarm assured her.

"Will I have any trouble finding a place to live?"

"Not a bit. There's plenty of rooming houses and little hotels right close to the downtown part, and was I you, I'd get a room in one of 'em. That'd make it easier to look for a job. Then, later on, you can rent a room by the week in a boarding house close to where you work."

"You seem awfully sure that I'm going to find a job without any trouble," Alila frowned.

"I am sure, Alila. And I'll keep my eyes peeled to see if I can help you."

For a moment Alila sat silent, then she said hesitantly, "I think I'd better tell you something, Longarm."

"I'm listening."

"My name's not Alila. It's really Alicia. Alicia..." She paused for a breath, then continued, "Alicia Jones."

Longarm looked at her, frowning, and asked, "How came you to change it? You ain't hiding out from somebody, are you?"

Alila—Alicia hesitated before saying, "I changed it when Mr. Tucker hired me at the Cowboy's Rest. He said Alicia wasn't fancy enough. The way he put it was that 'Alicia' might remind his customers of some girl they used to know. He told me the cowboys liked for dance-hall girls to have fancier names."

"It wouldn't surprise me if he was right," Longarm nodded. "I know I never did run into a dance-hall girl named Mary or Jane. But you didn't answer the rest of my question. Is there somebody out there looking for you?"

"I'm not sure, but I don't think so."

"None, what kind of answer is that?" Longarm frowned.

With a sigh, Alicia said, "It's the only kind I can give you, Longarm, because I really don't know."

"Why don't you start at the beginning and tell me what you're so afraid of?"

Again Alicia delayed her reply for a moment. Finally she said, "I ran away from my husband. He might be trying to find me, and I don't ever want to see him again."

"You're a married lady, then?"

"I guess that's what you'd have to call me," she nodded. "I never did file any divorce papers before I left the East, or anything like that. And, for all I know, my husband hasn't filed any, either."

"Would you be embarrassed if you told me what happened between you?" Longarm asked. "It might help to talk about it, sorta get your troubles off your mind."

"It's not much of a story," Alicia sighed. "And it's not very pretty."

"I don't guess there's many kinds of stories that I ain't heard, and most of 'em wasn't pretty. It'll do you good to get it off your chest."

"Maybe you're right," Alicia nodded. "And I suppose what happened between Sam and me isn't anything new." She fell silent again, her forehead knitted in thought, then went on, "I guess I just picked the wrong man to fall in love with. Or thought I was in love, at least."

"You wouldn't be the first one to make that kind of mistake, Alicia," Longarm told her consolingly.

"I guess not," she agreed. "Well, it didn't take me long to find out that Sam wasn't much more than a common loafer. He sponged on my family till I was ashamed and got a job myself. I rented us a flat, but Sam didn't lift a finger to earn money to pay the rent. I stood it a couple of months, and then packed up and left him. I kept my job, and was even able to put a little money aside, so when he found out where I'd moved to and began knocking on the door at all hours of the night, yelling for me to let him in, I decided to put as much country between us as I could. I didn't even tell my family, just packed what clothes I could get into a portmanteau and got on the train."

"And wound up in Ogallala," Longarm finished when she fell silent.

"Not all in one jump," Alicia told him. "I had some pretty bad times and did a few things I'm not proud of. But I did get to Ogallala, and then... Well, you know the rest of it."

Longarm nodded. "I don't see you've got anything to be ashamed of," he said. "You was just doing what you felt like you had to do."

"If I hadn't left, I'd've done something worse," she said. "And maybe I made a mistake in leaving the Cowboy's Rest. Mr. Tucker's a nice man, and he was good to us girls."

"Sure. But the way I see it, you're going to be better off in Denver," Longarm replied. "There's more—" He stopped as the locomotive whistle sounded and he recognized the meaning of its three short toots. He glanced past Alicia to look out the window. "We'll talk some more later on. You might like to look out and see what you think about Denver."

Alicia turned toward the window and watched as the scattered houses of the city's outskirts flashed past. Longarm stayed silent, not wanting to interrupt Alicia's absorption in the scene. The train's speed slackened to a crawl and then it stopped at the Union Station.

"Well, how does it look to you?" Longarm asked when Alicia finally turned away from the window.

"It looks so big I think I'm a little bit afraid, Longarm. Right now, I feel like I might've been wrong to leave Ogallala."

14

"Now, don't go borrowing trouble. You'll get along fine," Longarm assured her. He stood up and lifted Alicia's portmanteau off the luggage rack. "Come on. I been thinking about where you can likely find a room. I been with you this far; I might as well stick with you not till you get a place to stay."

"Whatever you say, Longarm," Alicia nodded.

Outside the Union Depot, Longarm hailed the first cab in the waiting line and told the hackie, "Take us down Eighteenth Street to Curtis and then sorta zigzag around eastwards between Curtis and Arapahoe and Champa till I tell you where to stop."

Like the hack drivers in any large city, this one was used to obeying orders from any fare who seemed to know the town, and he followed Longarm's instructions without blinking an eye. The neighborhood was one which had attracted well-to-do families in the city's earlier days. The houses they had built were large, two- and three-story structures, and as the city had spread as it grew the original owners had moved to the newer suburban areas and their homes had been converted into flats and rooming houses.

Alicia sat in silence, following Longarm's example, looking at the dwellings, until he saw a ROOMS FOR RENT sign and told the driver to pull up. Handing Alicia down from the hack, Longarm told the driver to wait. They went inside.

A tap-bell stood on a table by the door and its high-pitched *ping* brought the landlady to the hall. The room that she showed them was large and clean. It had a figured Wilton carpet on the floor, and the light from the single big window flooded it with brightness.

Though the furniture was old, it was well-cared-for. The landlady stood just inside the door while Longarm crossed the room to look out the window. Alicia moved around, examining the furniture, then came back to where Longarm waited.

"I think this will suit me just fine," she whispered. "I hope it's not too expensive."

Keeping his voice low, Longarm said, "I'd guess she'll ask you about fifteen dollars rent a month, so if I was you and could afford it, I'd say I couldn't afford to pay more'n ten and figure to get it for twelve."

He stayed by the window while Alicia went over and talked to the landlady briefly. When she returned, she told him, "You were right about her asking price, but I started by offering nine dollars and got the room for ten. I gave her a month's rent in advance, so I guess now I've got a home in Denver."

"That's good," Longarm nodded. "Now let's leave your bag here and go get something to eat. I'm just about starved."

They ate at a small cafe a short walk from the rooming house. The afternoon was still only half gone when they returned to the room.

"I guess I better go report in at the office," Longarm said.

"Isn't it awfully late for you to go to work? I was hoping you'd stay here a while and tell me more about Denver, where I ought to start in tomorrow, looking for a job."

Longarm thought for a moment and replied, "Well, it's getting on for late, all right. And I left my travelling gear in the baggage room at the depot. By the time I picked it up and got downtown, I might not be there before the office closed."

"Good," she smiled. "Now, let me help you take off your coat and be comfortable. Then you can sit down in that big chair and I'll take the little one and listen while you tell me where to go and ask for work tomorrow."

Alicia stepped up to Longarm and pulled the lapels of his coat apart. When she saw his Colt she gasped and took a step back without releasing her grip on the coat. Her unexpected move took him by surprise and he lurched forward, off balance. She threw her arms around him to help him steady himself, and Longarm involuntarily clasped her to him. Alicia turned her face up to look at him and their eyes locked for a moment. Then he bent down and their lips met in a long kiss.

It was Longarm who broke their embrace. He said, "I ought not've done that, Alicia. I ain't the kind of man that expects a woman to pay for a little favor."

16

"Don't you think I know that?" she asked. "I intended to try to get you to kiss me when I took off your coat. And, just to prove it . . ."

Alicia locked her fingers around Longarm's neck and pulled his head down. He didn't resist too strongly, and their lips met. This time their embrace was prolonged until both of them were breathless.

"I guess I better change my mind and go right now," Longarm told her when they broke the kiss.

"Please don't!" Alicia pleaded. "I've been wanting to kiss you all day, but I was afraid to make the first move. I'm not asking you to stay just as a way to pay you for helping me. Why do you think I asked you not to go to your office?"

"Why, I just figured you wanted company, being in a strange town and all."

"Your company, Longarm," Alicia replied. "Not just anybody who might be around. Don't make me beg you, please! Say you'll stay with me tonight."

"If you're sure—" he began.

"What do I have to do to convince you?" she asked.

Alicia pressed her body against Longarm and turned her face up, her lips pursed, inviting another kiss. Her confession had eased her mind, and Longarm responded by embracing her and bending down to join his lips to hers. Alicia ran her hand down his side and slid it between them. Longarm felt her fingers exploring his crotch, finding and then caressing him with gentle strokes and squeezes. He reacted as would any man who had been without feminine companionship for nearly a month.

"Oh, my!" Alicia breathed gustily as she broke their kiss, her fingers still caressing Longarm through the fabric of his trousers. "From the first time I saw you I was sure you were a lot of man, but I didn't expect all this much!" She stepped away from him long enough pull down the shade of the room's single window. Then she began to unbutton her blouse. "Hurry and get undressed! I've been without a man too long!"

Convinced by now that Alicia was not offering herself

17

as a thank-you gesture, Longarm undressed quickly, his eyes fixed on her. Enough light filtered through the drawn windowshade for him to see her clearly as she tossed her blouse aside and stepped out of her skirt.

Longarm stood motionless for a moment, gazing admiringly at her. Then Alicia extended her arms, inviting him. He covered the space between them with a single long stride, lifted Alicia in his muscular arms, and carried her to the bed. As he lowered her to the counterpane, Alicia grasped his wrist. As Longarm straightened up, she pulled him down to enter her.

"Don't move for a minute," Alicia whispered into Longarm's ear as he lay with his head resting on her shoulder.

"Whatever you say," Longarm replied. "I feel pretty good just like we are now."

Alicia remained motionless for a moment or two, then rolled her hips tentatively from side to side. Longarm responded with firmer pressure, and she moaned deep in her throat, a soft, undulating sound like the purring of a cat. When Alicia began twisting her hips faster, Longarm took her move as an invitation and began stroking slowly in deep measured thrusts, holding himself pressed firmly against Alicia's twitching body at the end of each deliberate penetration.

Alicia responded quickly. Her breathing grew gusty and ragged, and her body started trembling. "Hurry, Longarm!" she whispered urgently. "You're doing wonderful things to me! I love it, and I don't want you to stop, but I can't hold myself back much longer."

"Let go whenever you feel like it," Longarm told her. "And don't worry about me stopping, because I ain't about to."

He kept stroking with his steady rhythm. Alicia's trembling increased and her body grew taut as a bowstring. She was writhing almost constantly now, her hips undulating, her back arching as Longarm drove his long strokes to completion. Her low, garbled moans became whimpers of joy and grew louder as he kept up his rhythmic driving. Then she suddenly exploded into a frenzy of hip-jerking

18

and frantic, throaty cries as her body writhed and quivered.

Longarm waited until her movements began to slacken, then drove into her with a last long stroke and held himself pressed to her shuddering body. Her spasm passed its peak and her cries died away to gusty sighs, while her body softened and she relaxed and lay motionless.

Alicia wrapped her arms around Longarm and pulled his broad chest against her quivering breasts. Her lips invited him, and he joined her in a lingering kiss, a soft intertwining of tongues. They held the kiss until both of them were breathless, and as their lips drew apart Alicia sighed.

"Wonderful, wonderful!" she whispered. "I've never felt so good before! All I can think about is the next time."

"I ain't going to make you wait," Longarm promised.

He raised his hips and commenced stroking again, slow, measured penetrations until Alicia began to respond again. As she came back to life and started bringing up her hips to meet his thrusts, he began lunging in a quicker rhythm. Alicia was slower in reaching her peak this time, and Longarm did not hurry her. He maintained an even tempo until he felt her body growing taut before speeding up his pace.

Alicia responded in short spans of increased intensity, and when Longarm sensed that she was growing tired he drove harder and faster, to bring himself to his own climax. When Alicia's keening cries broke the silence of the darkening room, Longarm began driving in triphammer lunges.

He thrust faster and deeper as Alicia went into her final writhing frenzy, and drove to his orgasm with a flurry of short quick thrusts. Then he jetted and slowed to a few last draining thrusts while Alicia's soft body sagged beneath him. He buried himself into her with a final plunge before relaxing and falling forward on her soft trembling body and lying motionless, totally spent.

Darkness had entered the room by the time the pair stirred. Alicia cupped Longarm's chin in her hands and pulled his head down until their lips met. Their kiss was soft and gentle. It had none of the urgency of their earlier kisses, and was nowhere near as prolonged. Alicia sighed as their lips parted.

"I haven't been with all that many men," she said. "But now I know what a real man can do for me. Don't leave me alone tonight, Longarm. I know I'll sleep better if you stay."

"Well, I ain't in a hurry to leave," Longarm replied. "Go on and go to sleep, Alicia. I promise you'll find me here when you wake up."

Chapter 3

Longarm's eyes were bright, his cheeks were freshly shaved, and his snuff-brown hat was slanted at a jauntier angle than usual as he entered Denver's federal building the next morning. He climbed the marble stairs to the second floor and walked into the outer room of the U. S. District Marshal's suite. His first quick glance showed him that the door to Billy Vail's private office was closed and that Henry, the young, pink-cheeked clerk, sat at his desk in the outer room.

"You'd better have a good reason why you didn't show up yesterday," the youth said. "Marshal Vail expected you to report to him right after the train got in from Ogallala."

"Well, it's too bad I disappointed Billy, but I reckon he'll have got over it by now," Longarm replied. "I guess he's in his office?"

Without waiting for the clerk's reply, he crossed to Vail's door and opened it. The chief marshal looked up from his paper-strewn desk and frowned. "Where the hell did you get off to yesterday?" he asked. "That train you said you'd be on didn't take all this time to get here from Ogallala."

"Now, Billy, you know how hard a man works when he's following a crook on a cold trail. I figured you'd want me to come to work fresh instead of all frazzled out, so I took a couple of hours to look after some personal business."

Vail snorted. "I'd bet a stove-in derby to a brand-new Stetson that your personal business had something to do with a bed and a woman." Then he added quickly, "But that's your own affair. I'd counted on you showing up, because when I got your wire that you'd closed that Steamboat Springs case, I persuaded my old friend Will Travers to put off going back to Texas yesterday just so the two of you could have a little visit."

"I'm right sorry I didn't get here," Longarm said. "What's wrong with me and Will visiting today?"

"Travers had to get back to Austin in a hurry, so he took the early train."

"That's too bad," Longarm said. "Will Travers has been real helpful to me a time or two when I've had trouble down in Texas. You come down to it, he's about the only man in that old outfit of yours that I'd walk down a dark alley to shake hands with."

"You might not have to go into that alley," the chief marshal told him.

"Oh? How's that, Billy?"

"Maybe you'd better sit down," Vail said. "This case I'm giving you to handle is going to take you to Texas, and it'll take me a little while to explain it."

Longarm pulled up the red leather upholstered chair that was his favorite and sat down at the end of Vail's desk.

Vail went on, "I don't suppose you've heard that Will's been promoted to Ranger captain?"

"No, but I'm right glad he was. He's about the only Ranger I could ever get along with."

"Damn it, Long!" Vail exploded. "I wish you'd stop bad-mouthing my old outfit! The Texas Rangers are good lawmen, and I'm proud I used to be one!"

"Now, Billy, you know I didn't mean nothing personal," Longarm said, his voice carrying a carefully rationed portion of regretful apology. "Sure, I'll give you that the Rangers

22

do a good job, but they're hell on wheels as far as outside lawmen are concerned."

"Well, they've got their reasons," Vail snapped. "Back at the time I was with them, half the sheriffs and town marshals in Texas were crooked, and some of them didn't even try to hide it. It took the Rangers to get rid of them."

"I know the Rangers had a lot of housecleaning to do, Billy, but it'd seem to me like they could ease up a mite about being so hard-nosed with us federal deputies that ain't got a black mark against us in the Ranger's books."

"What makes you think you haven't got some black marks in their books?" Vail asked. "You've gotten crossways with them more than once, and you know it as well as I do."

"I figure I've done 'em enough good to get whatever black marks I had rubbed out," Longarm replied. "I helped 'em get back Santa Anna's gold, and I got back one of their men that the *Rurales* had locked up down in Mexico, and—"

"That's enough," Vail broke in. "I'm not going to waste any more time arguing with you. But if it makes you feel any better, Will Travers made a point of asking me to put you on this case, and I don't think he'll let his men step out of line as far as you're concerned."

"Oh, I can take care of myself, Billy. You oughta know that by now," Longarm said. "I won't be carrying no chips on my shoulders when I go down to Texas."

"I'll hold you to that," Vail warned. "Now, the Rangers have finally caught up with the Kiowa Kid, and—"

"Hold up, Billy!" Longarm broke in. "There ain't no way the Rangers could have the Kiowa Kid. If you recall, I've seen two Kiowa Kids buried, and now you say there's *another* one on the loose?"

"That's not so uncommon, Long," Vail replied. "There were about a dozen Billy the Kids at one time."

"Oh, sure," Longarm nodded. "Some smart-ass young-ster is always travelling under a famous outlaw's name. Then he gets his comeuppance and, after he's been dead a while, another crook picks up the name again."

"I know that, damn it!" Vail snapped. "And it's our job

to bring him in if he's committed some new crime."

"Now, the first Kiowa Kid I run into was killed and scalped by a renegade Sioux in the Indian Nation," Longarm said thoughtfully. "And the second one's been buried two years or so, and I'll lay odds he was the *real* Kiowa Kid. You oughta remember; I killed him myself in a shootout up in Dakota Territory, and seen him buried and covered up with six feet of dirt."

"I haven't forgotten," Vail replied.

"Then what am I going to Texas for?" Longarm asked. "You and Will sure don't think the Kid's pushed up through all that dirt and started outlawing again, do you?"

"No, of course not! What Will Travers thinks is that the Kiowa Kid you shot might not have been the real Kid at all."

"Oh, now, Billy! You think I'd have cut down on somebody I wasn't sure about? Don't forget, I took the Kiowa Kid prisoner about three months before we shot it out."

"I know that, Long," Vail said a bit peevishly. "And he got away from the prison guard that was taking him to the pen. That's why I had to send you out to run him down a second time."

"Which I did," Longarm put in. "I figured from the way he was moving that he was trying to get to Canada and circled around to head him off. He walked right into me up on Big Coulee Creek, and even after he seen I had my Winchester in my hand he went for his gun. I didn't have no choice but to kill him, and then I hauled his body over to the Standing Rock Indian Reservation to get him buried."

"I never did understand why you took all that trouble," Vail said. "You could've buried him yourself right where you brought him down."

"I had the best reason in the world, Billy," Longarm explained. "My slug taken the top of his skull off, and you know how that kind of shot twists a face all outa shape. When I'd stopped at the reservation earlier, while I was circling around, I found out there was a missionary there that had known the Kid down in Indian Territory. I wanted that missionary to look at the Kid's body so that if there was ever any question about who I'd shot he could swear it was the Kiowa Kid."

"And he did?"

Longarm nodded. "That's why I'm dead certain I got the right man."

"Everybody can make a mistake now and then," Vail pointed out. "Even if you and the missionary agreed it was the Kiowa Kid you'd shot, it might not have been. And anyway, regardless of whether he was the original one or not, Will Travers's Rangers have caught a Kiowa Kid way down in the southwest corner of Texas," Vail said.

"I still don't see where I fit in on all this," Longarm frowned.

"You're sure you shot the Kiowa Kid and watched him buried. Now, if you'll recall, we've still got a federal murder conviction against the Kiowa Kid. If the one that Travers is worrying about is the same one that escaped from the prison guard, he won't have to be tried again in Texas. The Rangers will just turn him over to you and you'll deliver him to the federal pen."

"Well, I got to admit that makes sense," Longarm nodded. "It'd save Texas a lot of money if they didn't have to bring him up in court."

"Exactly," Vail nodded. "And you're about the only one who can identify the original Kid."

"Which I can't do without taking a look at him," Longarm said resignedly. "And that means I got to get on another train and spend two or three days riding down to Texas just to look at whatever son of a bitch the Rangers have captured. Damn it, Billy, ain't that railroad that's pushing tracks up here from Texas ever going to get past Trinidad?"

"You mean the Fort Worth & Denver? I guess they're doing the best they can," Vail shrugged. "But until they get their tracks laid up here, there's nothing you can do about it, and the sooner you get moving, the better."

"Well, there ain't much for me to pack. I wound up at Bill Tucker's Cowboy's Rest up in Ogalalla, and you know how he fixes up his old customers, has their clothes washed and all."

Vail nodded, then asked, "How is Bill these days?"

"Fine. Said to tell you hello and for you to get up when you can spare time for a visit."

"I'd like nothing better," Vail said, waving a hand at the stacks of papers on his desk. "But every time I think I'm making some headway in clearing up my paperwork, I get a new batch in the mail from Washington."

Longarm dropped the butt of his cheroot into the spittoon at the corner of Vail's desk and stood up. "I'll get moving, then," he told the chief marshal.

"I'll wire Austin and tell Will Travers that you're on the way," Vail said. "If you take the night train to Trinidad, you ought to be reporting to him the day after tomorrow."

"And if his Rangers behaves theirselves and I don't run into some kind of trouble, maybe I can get back here in less'n a week. I sure don't aim to lollygag, Billy. There's a sight of other places I'd sooner be than Texas."

Longarm sat dozing in his seat in the Fort Worth & Denver day coach. His hat was pushed down over his eyes, and he seemed to be undisturbed by the whiffs of hot oil, smoke, and an occasional dusting of soot that drifted back from the locomotive into the half-open window at his elbow. He woke with a start and was on his feet before the echo of a sharp explosion from the head of the train broke through the low-pitched clicking of the wheels.

By the reflex action that had almost become instinct, Longarm's hand had started for his Colt. Before he could reach the pistol's butt, the rhythm of the train changed as it started slowing down. The screech of brakes reached his ears, and his brain overcame his instinct. A bit sheepishly, Longarm let his gun hand fall to his side and turned to look around the coach.

There were only four other passengers, all men, and they had leaped out of their seats, too. For a moment they stood still, gazing around the coach. Then one of them moved to a window and stuck his head out to look toward the head of the train.

"It looks like there's trouble up at the engine," he said.

26

"It's not a wreck, because the rails are clear ahead. I guess all we can do is wait and see what's wrong."

"I don't really give a damn what's wrong, because whatever it is, there's not a thing we can do to fix it," another one said, settling back into his seat.

Muttering agreement, the passengers sat down again. Longarm stayed on his feet. "Reckon I'll walk up the tracks to the locomotive and see what happened," he announced. "If any of you gents want to keep me company—"

"No, thanks," the man in the Stetson replied. "I'll just wait, too. The conductor will come back after awhile and tell us what it's all about."

Longarm walked to the end of the day coach and swung to the hard-baked ground. A cluster of men had formed at the front of the locomotive. As he got closer, he could see that the entire train crew must has assembled.

They were clustered around the steam cylinder at the head of the locomotive, and as Longarm got closer he heard one of them say, "No, damn it, Sam! There's not any way that cylinder can be fixed outside of the shops! Even if me or Sid knew how to fix it, we ain't got the tools or a cylinder to replace this one. It's busted all to hell, and we can't run on just one."

Though what he had overhead told Longarm the complete story of the breakdown, he walked on until he reached the group. As they saw him, the railroaders turned away from the engine and looked around. One of the blue-suited men started toward Longarm and, as he drew closer, Longarm read the word "Conductor" on the metal shelf above his cap's visor.

"I guess you're already figured out we've got a breakdown here," the conductor said.

"Sure," Longarm nodded. "I heard one of you say something about a cylinder busting."

"That's right."

He pointed to the bulging cylinder that almost hid the two front wheels of the 2-6-2 Prairie class locomotive. Wisps of steam were oozing from a crack that ran diagonally from the top of the casing and disappeared into its curving bottom.

As a frequent railroad passenger, Longarm had picked up enough knowledge of trains to see that the breakdown was indeed serious. He said, "Looks to me like we'll be here quite a while. If you don't mind, I'll just stick around a minute or two while you figure things out. My name's Long, Custis Long. Deputy U. S. marshal outa the Denver office."

"You can stay and welcome, Marshal," the railroader told him. "I'm Sam Knowles, the conductor. By the operating rules, I'm in charge of the train when it's standing still. If there's anything special on your mind..."

"Nothing special," Longarm said when Knowles's voice trailed off. "I was just wondering how late I was going to be showing up in Austin."

"I'm only guessing, Marshal Long, but I'd say you'll be at least a day late, maybe two. It'll depend on how fast we can get a crew and another locomotive up here from the division point. I'll know more about that as soon as I tap into the telegraph line over there and send a message to the division super, telling him what's happened to the train."

"Then I better step aside and let you get on with your business," Longarm said. "Don't pay no special attention to me. I'll just hand around here awhile, till you've finished your telegraphing."

With a nod, Knowles brushed past Longarm and swung up the steps to the baggage car. He came out a moment later carrying a pair of linesman's spurs in one hand and in the other a telegraph key, its dangling lead terminating in a wire-clip. He started walking along the right-of-way grade, heading for the nearest of the poles that supported the single strand of telegraph wire. After he'd taken a few steps, Longarm decided to follow him and look at the damaged cylinder later on.

Knowles strapped on the spurs and mounted the pole. He clipped the key to the wire and tapped out a message. After he had repeated the call twice, the conductor stopped sending, waiting for a reply. After several moments passed with no response, he repeated the code, waited again for a reply, then sent it once more.

28

"Now, it ain't none of my business, Mr. Knowles," Longarm called, "but I'd say you got a dead line."

"Yes, I've just about decided that," Knowles relied.

"Then I don't reckon there's much you can do about it, is there?"

Knowles has started climbing down the pole. He shook his head and said, "Not a thing. We're not due into Chilicothe—that's our next station stop—for another hour, and they won't get worried until the stationmaster realizes that something's wrong. I'd guess that'll be an hour or so after we're scheduled to pull in."

"It looks to me like the train won't get to Fort Worth till some time late tomorrow, then."

"I'd say that's a pretty good guess, Marshal, seeing it's the middle of the afternoon now," Knowles agreed. They started walking back to the locomotive. "Of course, Chilicothe's a division point, so as soon as they realize we're broken down, they'll send a crew up to help us regardless of what time it is."

"How far's Chilicothe?" Longarm asked.

"About fifteen miles."

"Now, you tell me if I'm wrong, but since you didn't get no answer when you tried to telegraph, that'd mean the line's busted between here and Chilicothe."

"That's right," the conductor nodded.

"You know, a man could walk fifteen miles in maybe two hours," Longarm suggested.

A thoughtful frown formed on Knowles's face. After a moment he said, "A man could get there in less time than two hours. It didn't occur to me until you asked about distances that we've got a section-hand shanty about two miles up the track. There's a handcar there, and with two men pumping it could get to Chilicothe in a little under an hour."

"You'll be sending somebody up there, then?"

"Of course. It'll save us a lot of time."

"Would you mind if I went along? Chances are the telegraph wire out of Chilicothe's all right, and I need to send a message to Austin. Captain Will Travers of the Texas

Rangers is looking for me to be there tomorrow."

" I don't have any objections at all. There'll be plenty of room on the handcar, if you don't kind walking to the shanty."

"That won't bother me a bit," Longarm told Knowles. "I'll just step into the coach and pick up my necessary bag and rifle. Then I'll come on up to the engine."

Carrying his small valise and his rifle, Longarm joined the train crew at the locomotive just in time to hear Knowles say to the engineer, "I don't argue that you need everybody in the crew to help you, Bob. But if only one man goes, he can't pump that handcar any faster than he could walk."

"It's going to be hard enough for five of us to take off that cylinder and piston shaft. With just three of us left here, there's not any way we can handle it," the engineer insisted.

Longarm stepped up to Knowles and said, "If it'll help, I'd as lief work my way on that handcar."

Knowles and the engineer exchanged glances, and both nodded at the same time. Then Knowles said, "Since Marshal Long's volunteered, I'd say your best bet is to send Simmons to Chilicothe." When the engineer nodded in agreement, the conductor turned back to Longarm and said, "We'll be glad to have your help, Marshal Long. You and Sid can start any time."

"I'm as ready as I'll ever be," Longarm replied. "And we ain't going to get nothing done if we stand here palavering."

"You're right about that," the fireman agreed. "Let's get moving, Marshal."

30

Chapter 4

After Longarm and Simmons had trudged along in silence for a quarter of an hour, Longarm began squinting ahead, trying to catch sight of the roof of the railroad shanty.

"We've got a good ways to go yet," Simmons told him.

"Well, I ain't been counting steps," Longarm replied. "I got a pretty good idea about distance, though, and I figure we oughta be about halfway by now."

Simmons was obviously unused to walking, for his stride was becoming a bit ragged, and he had started to pant even before they were out of sight of the train. The sky was clear and the day hot, and both men were sweating freely.

"If you feel like you need to stop and rest a minute or two, we ain't running no footrace," Longarm suggested.

"I'd as soon keep moving," the fireman replied. "The faster we get there, the sooner we'll be rolling along on that handcar. To tell you the truth, I'm not much good at walking. I can swing a coal scoop for a full shift without it bothering me, but the older I get, the more I appreciate riding."

As they moved on in silence, Longarm began slowing

his long, swinging strides, forcing his companion to a slower pace. When they reached the shanty, the fireman plodded down the slight grade from the roadbed and took a key from his pocket. When he swung the wide door open they saw the handcar resting on the little building's gravelled floor.

"I'm sure glad to see that," Simmons gasped. He went into the shanty, sat down on the deck of the handcar, then stretched out. "I've got to rest a minute before we wrestle this thing onto the tracks."

"Take your time," Longarm told his companion.

They rested in silence while the railroad man's panting subsided and Longarm puffed on a cigar. At last Simmons sat up and stretched. "If I lay here any longer, I'll go to sleep," he said. "If you're ready, we better wrestle this car onto the tracks and get started again."

"You're sure you rested enough?" Longarm asked.

"Oh, sure. Once we start moving on the handcar I'll be all right. I get tired walking because I don't do enough of it, but I can pump a handcar all day and all night; it's what I'm used to. Come on, Marshal. Let's get started."

The railroad man grasped the side of the handcar and had it raised off the ground while Longarm was still groping along the little vehicle trying to get a grip on it. To his surprise, the car was lighter than he had thought it would be. They toted it across the short gravelled rise to the tracks. To set the car on the rails they had to turn it at right angles. They lowered it carefully, then got on it and pumped the handlebars once or twice to make sure the car would move. Three or four sample pumps started it rolling, but before they'd gone more than a few yards Simmons signalled Longarm to stop.

"I've got to lock the shanty before we leave," he said.

"And I got to pick up my rifle and bag," Longarm told him. "But now we're ready to roll, let's don't waste no time."

They started toward the shanty, walking back beside the tracks, but before they had taken two steps a shot cracked from the high prairie grass and a slug kicked up a shower of gravel from the roadbed. To Longarm, being shot at was no novelty, and to fire back was almost instinctive. Before the gravel sent up by the rifle slug has fallen back to the ground he had his Colt in his hand and, though the sniper was hidden in the tall grass, he let off an answering shot aimed in the direction from which the rifle bullet had come.

Seeing a ripple in the grass that moved it against the wind, he followed it with another as he dropped down between the rails. He raised his head cautiously, looking for another sign that would betray the rifleman's position, but saw none. Simmons was still standing. He was looking around, trying to locate the direction from which the shot had been fired.

"Get down, damn it!" Longarm snapped. "You look like a flagpole on this flat prairie!"

Simmons was dropping to the roadbed just as a second shot whistled over their heads. Longarm rose to his knees. To give the unseen sniper something to worry about, he loosed two more slugs in the direction from which the rifle fire had come.

Simmons was lying on the road-grade, his head swivelling from Longarm to the prairie. His voice displaying his surprise, he asked, "Who'd be shooting at us? We haven't done anything!"

"I ain't got no more idea than you have," Longarm replied. "But whoever it is means business, or he wouldn't've let off that second round. Come on, let's crawfish behind that handcar where it'll give us a little bit of cover. It won't be much, but even a little bit's better than none at all."

As they began crawling, Longarm took four fresh shells from his coat pocket and swung out the cylinder of his Colt to reload. Simmons started to stand up and, before Longarm could speak or get even a single fresh cartridge into the Colt's cylinder, another shot cracked. Simmons dropped flat again. Longarm snapped the Colt's cylinder back into place and let off his last round.

A wild Indian whoop broke the still air. In spite of the danger, Longarm lifted his head in time to see a horse rise from the tall grass and a man swing into its saddle. Longarm realized he was a prime target. The rider brought up his rifle and got off another unaimed shot before reining his mount around and galloping off. Longarm had been trying to load his Colt by feel, his eyes on the horseman.

As the sniper started moving, Longarm kept his eyes on him, fumbling fresh shells into the revolver. He knew he would be too late to get off another round before the man was out of range. He stood watching the sniper gallop off, swinging his rifle in one hand. He mounted a small rise and disappeared on the downslope beyond.

"Ain't you going to shoot back?" Simmons asked.

"Why the hell should I?" Longarm replied. "That back-shooting son of a bitch was outa range of my Colt the first time he broke cover. He's got clear away, now. If I hadn't got careless and left my Winchester in that shanty, I'd bet a dime to a plugged penny I'd've had him, though."

"I can't understand why we didn't see him sooner," Simmons told Longarm. "There's no place for a man and a horse to hide on this bare prairie."

"Try on a buffalo wallow for size," Longarm said as he thumbed the last bullet into the Colt's cylinder and shoved the weapon into his cross-draw holster. "Likely he was an Indian; they got a way of making a horse lay so it don't make much more of a hump than a man. But I'd bet if we went to look at where he was, we'd find a buffalo wallow that he hid in when he seen us coming."

"Why do you figure he was shooting at us?" Simmons asked, his face furrowing into a puzzled frown.

"I'd give a lot to be sure, but at a guess I'd say, whoever that fellow is, he's on the run from something." Then, drawing on his experience, Longarm went on, "A man on the getaway gets nervous, Simmons. After awhile he figures anybody he runs into is hunting him, and he starts shooting wild."

"Do you think he'll come back?"

"Not likely. But I'd know him again if I see him with a rifle in his hand. There was something funny about the way he was holding it. I was too busy reloading too look at him good, but I'll bet a good silver dollar against a wormy apple that I'll know him next time I see him."

"You don't think he'll come back?" Simmons asked again.

Longarm shook his head. "He's long gone. And we better get moving too, and close up them miles between us and Chilicothe."

By pumping the handcar vigorously, Longarm and Simmons arrived in Chilicothe in the late afternoon. Simmons said, "I guess our best bet's to stop at the depot first. It's right at this edge of town; the shops are clear across on the other side."

"Stopping at the depot's fine with me," Longarm told him. "All I got to worry about now is sending a wire to Austin saying not to look for me until the day after tomorrow. I can worry about how I'll get there after I've got the message off my mind."

"You better add another day to when you'll be there," the railroader suggested. "As near as I can see, you won't get to Austin as soon as you've been figuring."

"I thought you told me Chilicothe's a division point," Longarm frowned. "Most railroads I know anything about keep a spare engine at division points in case there's a breakdown like this one that's holding me up."

"Well, the Fort Worth & Denver doesn't," Simmons replied.

"What about the passengers?" Longarm asked. "I'd say most of 'em are like me; they've got somebody waiting to meet 'em, wherever they're headed."

"Oh, I'm sure they have, and it's too bad they'll be late, but it can't be helped."

"Mind telling me why it's going to take so long?"

"Well, the station agent's going to have to send the work-donkey out to haul the flyer here, where they can work on it. I'd guess they'll use the donkey to get the drag on into Fort Worth, but it won't make as good time as the regular loco. I'd say for certain that you won't get there in time to make connections with the Katy for Austin."

Longarm nodded and joined Simmons in bearing down on the pump-bar to bring the handcar to a stop.

Picking up his rifle and bag, he followed Simmons to

the station door. The door was closed and locked, and when they walked down the platform to peer through the nearest window both the waiting room and the cubicle usually occupied by the agent were deserted.

"Something's wrong," Simmons frowned. "The agent's not supposed to shut up the depot as long as there's a passenger haul due to pass through."

"Maybe he just gave up when the train didn't pull in on time," Longarm suggested.

"If he's done a fool thing like that, it's going to cost him his job."

They had been walking around the perimeter of the platform while they talked. All the windows they passed were dark and the doors to the baggage room were closed and locked, as was the door on the opposite side of the depot. Longarm stepped to the edge of the platform and peered down the dirt street that led into Chilicothe's main and only business street. He turned back to Simmons.

"Looks to me like something's going on down the street," he said. "A bunch of people milling around like they was all excited about something. Maybe we oughta go see what's happening."

"I suppose we'd better. Maybe we can find out from somebody why the depot's closed up."

None of those in the milling crowd noticed the arrival of Longarm and Simmons. Longarm stepped up to a middle-aged woman standing at the edge of the sidewalk.

"Begging your pardon, ma'am," he said. "Maybe you won't mind telling us what's going on out there?"

She turned to look at Longarm and Simmons and asked, "You mean you ain't heard yet?"

"We just got here," Longarm explained.

"Why, they're still trying to get up a posse," she went on. "Only it seems like nobody wants to be in charge of it, and the marshal can't, because whoever it was that killed Cliff Little put a bullet in Linc's arm."

Suddenly the mysterious attack on the prairie made sense to Longarm. He said, "If you'll point out the town marshal, ma'am, I might be able to help him. You see, I'm a deputy

United States marshal, and I—"

He got no further than that. The woman whirled around and raised her voice to a shrill shout. "Linc!" she called. "Linc Sawyer! Hyper over here right quick! It looks like somebody's just come to town that can help you git that posse moving!"

The hubbub of voices in the street died away. The crowd had turned to look and from its center a man with one arm in a sling was pushing his way toward the sidewalk.

"You're a United States marshal?" Sawyer asked.

"Sure am," Longarm nodded. He spoke unhurriedly, his eyes and half his mind busy sizing up Sawyer. The Chilicothe marshal had seen the prime of his life ten years before, judging by his seamed and weatherbeaten face. "My name's Long, Custis Long. I work outa the Denver office."

"Long?" Sawyer repeated. "Long. Why, sure! I place you now. You're the one they call Longarm."

"I answer to that," Longarm said quietly. "Now, suppose you tell me what you're getting up a posse for, and I'll see if I can help you."

"Murder's why we're making up a posse, Marshal!" Sawyer replied. "Downright cold-blooded murder!"

"Who got killed?" Longarm asked.

"My night deputy, Cliff Little. He wasn't even on duty when he got killed. He was shot down without no reason at all, far as I been able to find out."

"You mean you don't know who done it?"

Sawyer shook his head. "Nobody seen it happen, as far as I been able to find out. There wasn't many people out, it being noon and most folks setting down to dinner."

"Then how'd you happen to get shot?" Longarm asked.

"I was coming up the alley from the livery stable when I heard the shooting. Then I heard a hoss starting off at a gallop and pushed between two buildings to get to Main Street. I got to the street in time to see some fellow riding hard outa town, and Cliff laying down on the ground across the street. The fellow on the hoss winged me before I could get my gun out."

"And your deputy was dead when you got to him?"

"So close to dying as makes no never-mind. Poor old Cliff just managed to get out two or three words after I got to him."

"What'd he say?" Longarm pressed.

"He gulped once," Sawyer replied. "Then he whispered, 'The Kiowa Kid.'"

Chapter 5

For a moment Longarm stared speechlessly at Sawyer. Then he asked, "Did you get the idea Marshal Little was telling you the Kiowa Kid shot him?"

"Sure," Sawyer nodded. "Wouldn't you get the same idea from what poor old Cliff said?"

"I guess I would," Longarm admitted. "Except I was sent out to bring the Kiowa Kid in a couple of years ago. When I caught up with him, he decided to shoot it out with me and lost. I buried him myself, up in Dakota Territory."

"That doesn't mean a lot, Marshal Long," Sawyer replied thoughtfully. "Back when I was spry enough to get around good, I ran across more than one owlhoot who'd borrowed another outlaw's name and reputation. I bet you've had that happen to you, too."

Longarm nodded. "But there's more to it than I've told you yet. Somebody that sure acted like an outlaw on the run taken a few shots at me and Simmons, here, up the railroad line a few miles."

"I'd be willing to make a good-sized bet that he was the

same one that killed Cliff," Sawyer said. "Everybody I've talked to that saw him agreed he was heading north when he made his getaway."

"From what you've told me, the time would be about right, too," Longarm frowned. "I figured him to be some kind of outlaw on the run, and now that you've brought up the Kid's name, I'd bet dollars to doughnuts it was him or whoever's borrowed his name. There's still one thing bothers me, though. How'd your man here know it was the Kiowa Kid?"

"Oh, Cliff covered a pretty good stretch of ground before he settled down here in Chilicothe," Sawyer replied.

"So he might've run across the Kid somewhere else?"

"Yep. He used to yarn a lot about the outlaws and killers he'd run across before he wound up here."

"It's funny I don't recall ever meeting Little," Longarm frowned. "I've covered quite a chunk of ground myself, but if we ever crossed trails I sure don't remember him."

"Cliff knew about you, Marshal Long," Sawyer said. "I've heard him mention your name more than once. Come to think about it, though, I can't call to mind that he ever said he'd known you, personal-like."

"Well, that's neither here nor there," Longarm told Sawyer briskly. "While we're wasting time jawing, whoever it was shot your deputy is making tracks outa this part of Texas as fast as he can, whether he was the Kiowa Kid or somebody else."

"There's a good reason why we haven't done much yet," Sawyer said. He patted the sling that supported his right arm. "This arm's not any use to me, so I've been getting up a posse to go after him. We were trying to figure out who ought to lead it when you showed up, but now that you're here, I can't think of a better man for the job."

Longarm shook his head. "Posses ain't my style, Marshal Sawyer. They're too noisy and slow and, when it comes to a shootout, they're as apt to kill one of their own people as they are the man they're after. Anyhow, this ain't a federal case, so rightly it ain't in my jurisdiction. What you want to do is get the Texas Rangers onto it."

40

"By the time we could get a Ranger here, that Kiowa Kid would be across the Red River into No-Man's Land or Indian Territory, and the Rangers would say that it's out of their jurisdiction, too," Sawyer said.

"Well, I'd like to get my hands on the Kiowa Kid," Longarm told the city marshal. "But I got strict orders to be in Austin soon as I can get there."

Sawyer was silent for a moment, then he said, "Regardless of your orders, you can't go on to Austin until the railroad gets moving again. Since you're going to be stuck here, and you say you want the Kiowa Kid, it'd make more sense to me if you put in your time trying to bring him in."

Longarm thought for a moment before answering, and the more he thought about it the more sensible Sawyer's suggestion looked. Even then he didn't reply to the old marshal at once, but turned to Simmons and asked, "How long you figure it's going to take for your railroad to start running on schedule again?"

"I can't say right this minute, but I might be able to in the next hour or so," Simmons replied. He pointed to a man on the edge of the crowd. "That's our station agent over there. As soon as I tell him what happened up the line, he'll wire the head office in Fort Worth and tell the general superintendent what happened. It'll take a little time for the super to get things worked out, but by early tomorrow morning—"

Longarm broke in on Simmons. "If I'm going to help these folks, I got to get moving right now. Just give me your best guess."

"You've lost most of today," the railroad man frowned. "My guess is you'll be stuck here for two more days."

Nodding, Longarm faced Sawyer again and said, "I'll tell you what, Marshal Sawyer. Even if I don't see how the killer that gunned down your night marshal can be the real Kiowa Kid, I sure want to get my hands on him."

"That means you'll help us, then?"

Longarm nodded, then said, "Like I told you a minute ago, I don't want no posse tagging along."

"That's up to you," Sawyer replied.

"I won't guarantee I can bring him in, of course," Longarm went on. "I've got till the day after tomorrow to catch up with him, but he's got half a day's start on me, and I ain't got a horse or saddle gear—"

Sawyer broke in, "Don't worry about that. I've got the best trail horse in these parts. He's mostly Morgan, but he's got some quarterhorse in him, so he's nimble and quick. I can fix you up with an outfit, too. Just tell me what you need."

"I guess I better have the whole rig," Longarm said. "I'm used to a McClellan saddle and, if your gear runs to a scabbard, my rifle's a Winchester .44. Saddlebags and a blanket or two'll just about finish out my list."

"I'll have everything you need in less than half an hour," Sawyer promised. "And if there's anything more..."

Longarm shook his head. Then, as an afterthought, he told the town marshal, "There's just one thing that bothers me. I don't know this part of the country as good as I'd like to. The other cases I've had in the Texas Panhandle has been further north, up around Mobeetie and Tascosa."

"Don't worry about that, either," Sawyer said quickly. "If you want somebody to go along and guide you, I've got a youngster eighteen years old that knows the lay of the land around here better'n most of us and ain't scared of a thing."

"Then I'll take you up on that, too," Longarm agreed.

"Just tell me when you want to start," Sawyer went on, "I'll have my kid down here with everything you need."

Longarm glanced at the sun. It was hanging low in the western sky by now. "I've got to send a telegram to Austin," he said. "That won't take long. You just go ahead and get your youngster primed to go with me, and put together gear and grub, and I'll be at the depot by the time you get back."

As the town marshal turned to go, Simmons told Longarm, "I caught the station agent's eye a minute ago. He's pushing up toward us now, so you won't have to wait to send your telegram."

"That's good," Longarm said. "I'll want to leave my

42

valise and this coat I got on at the depot; they'd just be in my way on the trail."

"Sure. And, if there's time, the agent might be able to find out when traffic will be back to normal on the line. If you know before you leave when the next southbound train's going to pass through, you can be sure you get back in time to catch it."

Back at the depot, Longarm opened his valise and took out a supply of ammunition for both his Colt and his Winchester, his stock of cheroots, and a box of matches. He put them aside to go into his saddlebags, folded his coat carefully, and tucked it in the valise. Then he went across the room to the station agent's counter, where Simmons and the agent were huddled by the clicking telegraph key. Simmons looked around as Longarm opened the counter flap and came into the little enclosure.

"I don't have the final word for you," he told Longarm, "but I'd say you'd better figure on it being three days. There's not a spare locomotive in the Fort Worth roundhouse, and not much chance of getting one from the Katy or the Rock Island."

"I sort figured that'd be the way of it," Longarm nodded. "So, if that wire ain't cleared before I ride out, I'll ask you to send a message to Captain Will Travers at the Ranger headquarters in Austin. Be sure to tell him what's held me up, and say that as soon as I get back here to Chilicothe I'll send him a wire and let him know when I can get there."

"I'll be glad to, Marshal," Simmons replied. "Now, is there any other way I can help you?"

"Nothing that comes to mind, except you might ask the station agent here to look after my valise till I get back."

A clattering of hoofbeats sounded outside the depot. "That'll be Marshal Sawyer and his youngster, which means I got to go."

"Good luck to you," Simmons said, extending his hand.

"And the same to you," Longarm answered.

Carrying his rifle and the necessities he'd taken from his valise, Longarm started for the depot door just as Linc

43

Sawyer opened it and came in.

"Here, let me give you a hand," Sawyer said. As he took the boxes of ammunition and the bundle of cheroots he went on, "I loaded your saddlebags pretty good with grub, so you won't be worried about starving. I'll just put this stuff in on top of the bags while you get acquainted with my youngster."

Two horses were standing with their reins tossed over the hitch rail outside the depot. One fit the description of the part-Morgan the town marshal had told Longarm about. Beyond it was a chestnut with the high arched neck and heavily muscled legs that showed it had a strong strain of Tennessee walking horse somewhere in its ancestry.

Both animals had empty saddles, and Longarm wondered where Sawyer's youngster had gone. Then he saw a pair of booted legs under the Morgan and realized that the rider of the chestnut was bending down between the two mounts, probably adjusting a stirrup strap. He slid his Winchester into the saddle scabbard and was just starting to walk around the horse to introduce himself to his travelling companion when Sawyer reached the hitch rail.

"Where in tunket did my—" he began.

From between the horses a light, youthful voice broke in. "I'm right here, Dad. Had to fix a loose stirrup cinch."

The speaker straightened up and Longarm's jaw dropped in surprise. Sawyer's youngster was a young woman.

"This is your youngster?" he asked Sawyer.

"Why, sure." Sawyer turned to his daughter and went on, "I want to make you acquainted with Deputy U. S. Marshal Long, Tina. He's the one you've heard so much about, the one that everybody calls Longarm. Marshal Long, Tina's right name is Christina, but nobody calls her anything but Tina."

Longarm doffed his hat. "I'm pleased to meet you, Miss Tina. I don't guess I need to tell you I was surprised to see you was a pretty young lady. When your daddy said he'd ask you to go along with me, he just called you a youngster."

"Yes, that's Dad's way, Marshal Long," she said. "And you might feel like changing your mind about me going

44

with you, now that you've seen me."

Sawyer broke in, "Now, Longarm, don't you make the mistake of thinking that Tina won't be much help to you just because she ain't a boy. I'll guarantee you, she can hold up her end of a job, all right. She can fork a horse almost as good as I used to, she's a good shot, and she's spryer than I was at her age."

"Don't pay any attention to Dad's bragging, Marshal Long," Tina said. "But if you still want me to go with you, now that you've seen me, I'll promise not to get in your way and I'll try to help you all I can."

Longarm had been studying Tina, not bothering to conceal his quick but close scrutiny. She was a tall girl, almost matching his own height. She wore a flat-topped *vaquero* hat, and he noted a few wisps of black hair curling below its brim. Her face was slender and her high-bridged nose matched its slimness. She had high cheekbones that tapered to generous, shapely lips and a narrow but firm chin. Full, straight eyebrows set off her dark eyes, eyes so dark that they were almost an opaque black. She was wearing a blue denim shirt that hung loosely from her shoulders and was tucked into tightly fitting covert-cloth riding breeches.

Although Longarm's inspection had taken only half a minute, Tina had been aware of its thoroughness.

"Well?" she asked, her voice level. "Do I measure up, Marshal Long?"

"I'd imagine you and me can get along all right," Longarm nodded. "But I wish you had on a pistol-belt with a Colt in the holster. There ain't no way of telling what we'll run into."

"I've got one in my saddlebags," she said, "and Dad taught me how to use it. But when I'm in the saddle, I've found that it's faster and easier to use my rifle."

"That makes good sense," Longarm agreed. "So, if you feel like you can put up with me for a day or two, we might as well get started."

"Good," Tina nodded. She planted a quick kiss on her father's cheek, went to her horse, and swung into the saddle.

In a low voice, Sawyer said to Longarm, "I know you'll

look after her all right, Longarm. I set a lot of store in Tina, but I wasn't going to let you ride out without the best help I can give you."

"Was I you, I wouldn't worry too much," Longarm told the old lawman. "I wouldn't've let your girl ride with me if I figured we'd get into a shooting scrape. We're starting out so far behind that fellow your deputy called the Kiowa Kid that we ain't got much chance of catching up with him."

"Sure," Sawyer nodded. "But you take good care of her, just the same."

Longarm nodded as he mounted and wheeled his horse. Tina had already turned the chestnut gelding and was sitting waiting for him a few yards away. When she saw him in the saddle, she toed her horse into motion, and Longarm nudged his own mount ahead to catch up and ride beside her.

After they had covered a short distance, Longarm said, "Your daddy told me you know the lay of the land hereabouts, so you'll likely know where that railroad shanty is, up ahead."

"Of course I do. Is that where you want to start, Marshal Long?"

"I ain't real sure, but before we get any further, I better tell you I don't cater much to titles. I got a sorta nickname—"

"Yes, I know," Tina broke in. "Longarm. I've heard Dad mention you a time or two."

"Well, since we're going to be riding together a few days, it'll be a lot friendlier if you'll call me by it."

"If that's what you want me to do, Longarm."

"That sounds better," Longarm told her. "Now, like I started out to say, when that sniper that had me and Simmons pinned down rode away, he was heading east and a little bit north. The way I figure, we'd be wasting time if we backtrack to the shanty to pick up his trail. What's the land like in the direction he was moving?"

"Plain flat prairie for about the first six miles," Tina said promptly. "And unless he turned north or south before then, he'd run into Settler's Draw two or three miles before he got to the Red River. Why?"

"Well, I've had plenty of time to think about where he was most likely headed, and I figure he was beelining for Indian Territory. It ain't all that far from the railroad shanty to the Red River, and the Territory starts across the Red, so we can be pretty sure he wouldn't move south. That'd take him back toward Chilicothe, and he'd want to make it to the river as fast as he could, so chances are he'd go due east."

"If he knows the country around here, he wouldn't try to cross Settler's Draw to get to the river," Tina frowned.

"Pretty rough, is it?"

She shook her head. "Flat and sandy and not much brush, but there's a little creek winding through that draw. It doesn't carry much water, but there's quicksand all over the place."

"Let's have a look at, then," Longarm said. "Sandy soil holds hoofprints real good. We might just pick up that killer's tracks a lot quicker than he'd be figuring anybody could."

Chapter 6

"Well, there it is," Tina said as she and Longarm reined in at the edge of a ragged ledge that dropped almost vertically into a broad expanse of reddish sandy soil. "Settler's Draw."

They were looking at one of the depressions so common to the arid southwest, too shallow and covering too great an expanse to be called either a canyon or a ravine. There were hidden pockets of quicksand here and there. Any unwary creature, man or animal, which was heavy enough to break through the crust soon sank out of sight and drowned in the semi-liquid contents of the hidden pocket.

"Do you know where all the sinks are, Tina?" Longarm asked.

Tina shook her head. "Nobody does. I know where some of the biggest ones are, but there are dozens more big enough to trap a horse, and I suppose a hundred more that could swallow up a man. I know one thing: I wouldn't want to cross this draw by myself."

How far do you figure we are from that railroad shanty right now?"

"Not more than six or seven miles." She pointed at an oblique angle to their position and told him, "The railroad shanty's in that direction. If the Kiowa Kid cut a beeline from the shanty to the draw, he'd have gotten to it a little bit north of where we are now. If he's heading for the Indian Territory he'd have had to go north anyhow."

Longarm glanced at the sky. He said, "It's too late for us to try crossing this stretch today, but we've still got an hour or so of daylight left. That's time enough to circle part of the way around it and see if we can pick up his tracks."

"Wouldn't it be smart for us to split up and ride along the edge of the draw in different directions?" she asked.

"You got a lot of trail sense, Tina," Longarm nodded. "And I figure just like you do. The big question is how good he knows the lay of the land around here, and all we can do is guess which way he headed after I lost sight of him. Have you got any druthers about which way you go?"

"No," Tina replied. "North or south, it's all the same to me. The only thing I care about is running down whoever murdered Uncle Cliff."

"I'll go north, then, and you go south."

"We'd better arrange a signal," she suggested. "A rifle shot carries a long way here on the prairie. If we find his tracks we can signal with a shot or two."

"How about one shot if we give up and quit, two shots if we run across his tracks?" Longarm suggested. "One shot means we're going to ride back and meet someplace close to where we are now, but whoever fires two shots will just stay put and wait for the other one to turn around and keep riding till they meet up with whichever one done the shooting."

"That sounds fine," she agreed, nudging her horse's flank with her boot toe. "I'll be on my way, then."

Longarm reined the Morgan in the opposite direction. They moved apart, tiny figures in a broad sweeping landscape under the descending sun.

Since the day's end was near and his horse would have a full night's rest, Longarm kept the half-Morgan moving at a distance-eating canter. He glanced over his shoulder at

Tina once or twice and once saw her turning to look back at him. They drew apart swiftly and were soon out of sight of each other.

As he rode, Longarm kept his eyes fixed on the rim of the sink. At most places it was very irregular and quite sharply defined. Occasionally the high ground descended to the floor in a gentle, ramplike slope.

It was as though he was riding along the border of two different countries. The high grassed prairie on his left was as level as though someone using shears had trimmed each stalk to the same height, while the draw on his right had been left untouched. The lower ground-level of the draw enabled him to see much farther across it and everywhere he looked it was broken by bare humped hillocks, small depressions, or level stretches, with isolated clumps of scrubby brush punctuating the untamed expanse.

Old son, Longarm told himself as he rode, *you got about as much chance as a snowball in hell of catching up with that killer.*

After he'd ridden about half a mile farther, Longarm's sagging hope suddenly vanished and was replaced by high expectation. He was approaching one of the places where the sheer wall of the draw was broken by a gentle downslope. On the slanting surface of the bare earth a set of hoofprints showed clearly, outlined by the rays of the low-hanging sun.

As he covered the short distance that remained between him and the rim's broken edge, Longarm studied the prints carefully. Following them with his eyes, he could soon see the small patch of disturbed and broken grass that marked the spot where the horse and rider had left the level prairie. He reached the slant and stood up in his stirrups. Even from that small elevation he could trace the swathe of broken, disturbed grass the rider had left across the prairie in approaching the draw. As nearly as he could tell, if he were to backtrack along the path, sooner or later he would arrive at the railroad shanty where the bushwhacker had fired on him and Simmons.

You picked up his trail for sure, old son, he told himself as he settled back into his saddle. Pulling his Winchester out of the saddle holster, he lifted its muzzle to the sky and triggered the two shots he and Tina had agreed on as their signal. He lighted a cheroot and through the cloud of blue smoke raised by his puffing peered at the angle of the sun's reddening pre-sunset rays. *Maybe she'll get here in time for us to track him a little ways before it get too dark to see,* he thought.

As his eyes followed the trail of prints left by the bushwhacker's horse, Longarm grew increasingly impatient. He could make out the U-shaped dents across the draw for perhaps a hundred yards before he lost sight of them on the rough ground where the slanting earth merged with the bottom of the sink. Beyond that point, the prints merged with the broken, clodded ground.

It won't do a bit of harm was you to follow them prints a little ways, old son, he told himself. *Tina'll see your tracks and come trailing along, and the more of that trail we can cover now, the less there'll be to follow tomorrow.*

As always, Longarm made his decision quickly. He picked up the reins and nudged the horse's flank. The half-Morgan moved at an easy walk down the slope and started across the floor of the draw. The hoofprints of the fleeing outlaw veered from a string-straight line only when he had had to curve around one of the small infrequent patches of sparse-limbed brushes.

It was when the gelding was detouring around one of these brush clumps that Longarm heard the buzzing of a rattlesnake warning that it was ready to strike and felt the gelding's instant reaction as it gathered its muscles to buck.

Longarm did not have time to wish he was in a stock saddle instead of a McClellan, which had no saddlehorn he could grab. He had been holding the reins loosely in his left hand and he locked his fingers on them while pulling in his knees, squeezing them against the slick leather of the front saddle pommel, while he swept his Colt from its cross-draw holster as the horse's hooves left the ground.

Even while the half-Morgan arced into its buck, Longarm's eyes were searching the brush clump, looking for the snake. He found it before the rattler's tail quit vibrating in preparation for its strike.

Triggering the Colt, he saw the snake's head fly off its writhing body. But the horse was now descending, turning in mid-air. The yanking of only one hand on the reins was not enough to quit its frenzied moves. Longarm dropped his pistol to grab for the reins with his right hand, but the whipping leather strips eluded his reaching fingers.

As he reached to grasp the flailing reins, he was forced to relax the precarious grip of his knees against the pommel. The horse landed with a jarring thud and, even though the ground under its hooves was soft, the impact almost sent Longarm tumbling to the ground.

Longarm's crotch hit the saddle hard as the horse landed. He felt the animal's back begin to arch in readiness for another leap. As quick as his reactions were, he was unable to slip off the saddle before the horse's hooves left the ground in another hard buck.

Longarm had lost his seat in the saddle and the animal was rising again before he could regain his equilibrium. He felt himself lifting from the saddle and rising into the air. His flailing arms knocked off his hat almost at once and he sailed for a dozen feet before he landed sprawling on the soft, yielding soil surrounding the clump of bushes.

For a moment, Longarm lay motionless, his arms outspread and his legs sprawled wide, before he realized that he had not felt the hard, painful jarring he had anticipated from such a fall. Then he stirred and felt the soft ground quiver beneath him. He started to raise himself on his elbows and felt the ground give way as his arms took the weight of his body.

Old son, you're laying in quicksand, he told himself. He sank back to distribute his weight over as large an area as possible. He had a fleeting moment of panic as his legs began sagging and his entire body continued to sink.

By exercising all the strength his sinewy muscles possessed, Longarm brought his body erect. As he straightened up, the quicksand released his shoulder and torso and he was able to pull his arms out of its grip. The surface of the clammy puddle was not at the joint of his hips, but he was still sinking.

Letting his knees bend and relaxing his torso slowed the rate at which he was sinking, but when he pushed one foot down to feel for bottom, he found nothing solid underfoot. By trying to lift himself he had speeded up the rate at which the pool of quicksand was engulfing him. He let both knees relax and bend and his sinking slowed perceptibly.

Longarm had been too engrossed in trying to free himself to give any thought to his horse. Now the half-Morgan tossed its head and nickered, drawing Longarm's eyes. The horse was a good ten feet away from him, standing on solid ground. He puckered his lips to whistle the animal to him, but in the split second before whistling Longarm realized that if the horse responded and stepped into the quicksand, it would be foundering in the bog with him before he could grab the reins.

Damned if you ain't in a real mess this time, old son, he told himself. *There ain't no way you're going to get out of this quicksand by yourself.*

He glanced at the sun. The bottom of its disc was already touching the rim of the draw, and its hue was no longer gold, but the deep red that signals the start of sunset. Very conscious of time now, Longarm realized that the thin, biting wind which springs up to accompany a summer sunset had already started blowing.

Suddenly he remembered something that he had forgotten. He had fired two shots to signal Tina to turn back and follow his trail until they met. Then he had fired a third shot at the rattlesnake. A single shot was the signal for Tina to wait for him to join her at the place where they had separated.

It's too bad you never did learn how to pray worth a damn, old son, he told himself grimly. *If Tina mistook your signal and stopped to wait for you, you'll be sucked plumb outa sight in this muck. Even if she's on her way here now, she might not get this far till you've sunk plumb outa sight.*

53

If any getting-out of this scrape is going to be done, you'll have to do it, so you might as well get started.

Even during the few moments since he had stabilized his position, the quicksand had reached his midsection. The half-dozen feet that separated him from solid ground seemed like fifty. He studied his surroundings, trying to find a way to pull himself out. Swimming came to his mind first, but his slow, careful movements only caused him to go deeper. The surface of the sand had now reached his beltline and was creeping up faster as more of his body sank.

"Was you the praying kind, old son, you'd be hunkering down on your knees right now," he said aloud. "The hell of it is, you ain't got nothing to kneel on. And even if—" He broke off as distant hoofbeats reached his ears. Releasing a long breath, he went on, "Maybe you been praying all the time and you just didn't know it. That sounds like Tina riding up." Raising his voice he shouted, "Tina!"

A faint shout reached him as Tina replied. He called again, "Hurry up, Tina! Just be careful to stay right over the tracks I made coming in here!"

He heard Tina repond again and the drumming beat of her horse's hooves increased in tempo. Within three or four minutes he saw her galloping toward him, but during those short minutes Longarm's sinking had accelerated. The quicksand's surface was now lapping at his upper vest pockets.

Tina started reining her horse when she saw Longarm's mount standing riderless beside the clump of brush. She pulled the chestnut to a halt, and looked around bewildered for a second before catching sight of Longarm's head and shoulders sticking out of what appeared to be solid ground.

"You're in quicksand!" she gasped. Then, without stopping to ask questions, she reached for the lariat that was hanging on the pommel of her saddle. She twirled the lariat into a small loop and, after swinging it twice, dropped the loop within Longarm's reach.

"Put it under your arms," she said. "And just keep still while I'm pulling your back to solid ground."

54

"You be careful, too," he said. "That ground you're on now's solid enough, but if you back up too far your horse might step into another bog and then we'd both be in the soup."

"Don't worry," she assured him. "Old Buck won't put his hoof down hard unless he feels firm ground under it."

While she spoke, Tina was throwing a double-twist loop of the lariat around her saddlehorn. She began backing the chestnut slowly. For a long moment after the rope began cutting into Longarm's chest, he did not move. Then he felt himself being dragged down as the tension on the lariat increased, and he threw his head back to avoid its being pulled under the quicksand's roiled surface.

Tina did not let the lariat go slack. She halted her horse, and Longarm found that he could wrap his hands around the rope and push his shoulders up to keep his face above the surface. He told Tina, "I can hang on this way if you got any more backing-up space."

"A little bit. Not much," she replied, glancing over her shoulder.

"Maybe a little bit's enough," Longarm said. "Another foot or so and I can pull myself hand over hand to where the ground gets solid."

He felt himself sinking once more as Tina inched her horse back once more, and he started pulling himself hand over hand toward the edge of the quicksand. Tina jumped from her saddle and ran up to help him.

"Stand, Buck!" she commanded the horse.

The horse remained motionless. Tina felt her way to the edge of the solid ground, testing its stability with the toe of her boot, until she reached the sink's edge. Leaning forward, she extended her free hand to Longarm.

He was only mid-thigh-deep now, and when he grasped Tina's hand and she joined her strength to his, Longarm's legs and feet slowly emerged. He kicked mightily, Tina synchronized her pull with his, and Longarm landed on firm soil.

For a moment the only thing either of them could do was

sigh with relief. Then Longarm said, "I sure owe you, Tina. If it wasn't for you, I'd be dead down at the bottom of that sink, if it's got a bottom."

"You don't owe me anything, Longarm. I'm just glad I got here in time. When I heard that third shot you fired, I decided something had happened that caused you to change our plan. I was going to stop and wait for you."

"What made you change your mind?" Longarm asked. He groped at his top vest pocket and found that he hadn't sunk deeply enough in the quicksand to wet his cigars. He took out one of the cheroots and a match and lighted up.

Tina went on, "You weren't where we were supposed to meet, so I just kept moving, thinking we'd meet each other a little farther along. I couldn't see you on the trail ahead, so I thought I might as well keep going and meet you. Then, when I saw the hoofprints where you'd started down into the draw, I began wondering if you might've run into trouble. I followed the prints and, when I heard you yelling, I speeded up."

"It's good thing you did," Longarm told her. "Another couple of minutes and I'd've sunk outa sight."

"Why did you fire that third shot?" Tina frowned.

"The horse got spooked by a rattlesnake and bucked me off when I shot the rattler. Then I was fool enough to move too fast when I tried to get out."

"Well, as it turned out, all you did was get your clothes soaked and full of sand," she smiled. "But I imagine you've got a change of clothes in your saddlebags, so as soon as you change we can start moving again."

While they talked, the sun had disappeared and the quick-gathering prairie night was near. He said, "I better wait till we get back on firm ground, Tina. This ain't no safe place to camp, and I'd as soon not try to keep on that trail back up to solid ground in the dark."

"You've picked up the Kiowa Kid's trail?" she asked.

"Near as I can tell," Longarm nodded. "But we got to be moving. It'll be plumb dark if we stay here jawing any longer."

Walking a bit stiffly because of the quicksand which had

flooded into his jeans and longjohns, Longarm stepped over to where his Colt had fallen and shoved it in his holster. By the time he got to his horse, Tina had already mounted. With Tina following him, he led the way to the safety of higher ground through the deepening gloom.

Chapter 7

When they reached the trail that ran around the rim of the draw Longarm reined in. "I guess this is as good a place as any to stop for the night," he told Tina. Pointing to a patch of low-growing mesquite a few yards ahead, he went on, "That little clump of brush over there oughta suit us. It ain't shelter, but it'll give us something solid to tether the horses to."

Tina nodded. "We're not likely to find anything closer, and the horses need rest as much as we do."

As they turned their mounts and nudged them ahead, Longarm went on, "It's a cussed shame to let that killer get any more of a lead on us, but we'd be plumb fools if we tried to cross that draw in the dark. I had all the quicksand I want for a while."

"I didn't realize there was quicksand there or I'd have mentioned it to you," she replied, reining in and swinging off her horse. "And I know you can't be very comfortable in those wet clothes."

"They're just about dry now," Longarm said as they

began unsaddling their horses. "Anyways, I ain't made outa sugar. I won't melt away."

"All the same, you'd better change into something dry. You can do that while I fix our supper."

"Now, I didn't bring you along to cook for me," Longarm protested. "I've got rations in my saddlebag."

"Jerky and parched corn?"

"How'd you know that?"

"Because it's what just about everybody carries." As she spoke, Tina was taking a cloth-wrapped bundle from her saddlebags. "Before I left the house I cut some slices off a roast of beef and wrapped them up with the biscuits left from noon, and a couple pieces of cake I baked yesterday. So you can save your corn and jerky for later."

"You didn't need to do that, Tina," Longarm protested.

"But I did, anyhow. So, while I get busy, you can change." Tina took her bundle and started toward a relatively clear spot a few feet off the trail.

Longarm had brought no extra trousers or boots. Sheltered between the tethered horses, he unwound his spare balbriggans from the bottle of Tom Moore that he'd bought in Denver, knowing that Texas was bourbon country. He pulled the cork and swallowed a healthy swig, then replaced the bottle in the saddlebag. What he had taken to be a vagrant breeze was turning into a series of gusty blows that showed no signs of diminishing, and Longarm hurriedly stripped off his wet clothes. He folded the wet balbriggans into a makeshift towel and, before putting on his dry pair, scrubbed himself vigorously until he had scraped away the grains of sand that still clung to his moist skin.

Since he had no other trousers, he shook the sand as best he could from the pair he had been wearing and slid his long legs into them. He donned a dry shirt, then cleaned his boots inside and out and managed to shove his feet back into them. He found a handful of stones, spread his wet shirt and underwear in a spot where the grass was sparse, and weighted down the garments, then went to rejoin Tina.

She had unfolded the tablecloth in which the food had been wrapped and laid their food on it. In addition to the things she had mentioned, there were also three boiled potatoes, an earthenware crock of preserves, and a tin cup filled with butter.

"I hope you've got a knife," she said as Longarm walked up. "I was in such a hurry that I forgot we'd need utensils."

Longarm took out his pocketknife and opened it, then passed it to Tina. She began slicing the potatoes. "It was real thoughtful of you to think about this grub, Tina, but you didn't need to go to a lot of trouble," Longarm told her.

"It wasn't any trouble," she protested. "All the food was cooked. The only thing I did was wrap it." She picked up a slice of meat and a chunk of potato and was ready to start eating when she noticed that Longarm hadn't helped himself. "Don't you like roast beef and potatoes?" she asked.

"Sure I do, better'n most things. But I was just thinking I'd like something to drink while I eat."

"So would I," Tina said. "If I'd known the wind was going to come up this way, I'd have brought a coffeepot and some coffee. A cup would sure taste good right now."

"If you ain't temperance, I got a bottle of good whiskey in my saddlebags," Longarm suggested. "It'll warm you up a lot better than coffee."

If you knew my dad better, you'd know he didn't raise any temperance children. I'd like a swallow of your whiskey, Longarm."

Longarm went to his saddlebags and came back with the bottle of Tom Moore. He pulled the cork and handed Tina the bottle. She tipped it back and swallowed, then gasped as she lowered it.

"That's a real tough whiskey!" she said.

"It takes a little getting used to, all right," Longarm agreed. He took a drink and offered the bottle to Tina again, but she shook her head.

"That was all the drink I needed," she told him. "Not that there's anything wrong with my appetite."

They ate quickly, with little conversation, and Tina began wrapping up the leftover food while Longarm lighted a cigar.

Night had closed in while they were eating, a moonless prairie night.

"It's been a pretty long day for both of us," Tina said. "I don't know about you, but I'm ready for bed."

Longarm looked at the glowing tip of his cigar and replied, "Me, too. We might as well fix a place to bed down while I'm finishing my cigar."

They moved to the edge of the mesquite and trampled down the tall prairie grass, seeking hidden rocks that would gouge them through their blankets, opened their bedrolls, and spread them several feet apart. Tina levered out of her boots and slipped between her blankets. Longarm stepped over to his saddle to get his Winchester, put it beside his blankets, and took off his gunbelt. He placed the Colt where it would be within easy reach and began taking off his boots.

"Goodnight, Longarm," Tina said through the gloom.

"'Night, Tina. See you in the morning."

Longarm's trousers began to feel clammy after he had gotten between his blankets and was sheltered from the cool wind. He slipped the trousers off and pushed them to the foot of his bedroll. After a few minutes he started feeling warm enough to take off his shirt and fold it up to use as a pillow.

Longarm had no idea how long he had slept when he felt on his cheek a touch as light as the falling of a flower's petal. He was awake instantly, aware of the form that blocked the stars and the warm flesh his groping hand had encountered before it reached the Colt.

"Tina?" he asked.

"Yes. I don't know why, maybe I heard a strange noise, but I woke up with a start a few minutes ago. Did you hear anything, Longarm?"

"Not a thing. What'd the noise sound like?"

"I—I don't really know. I'm not even sure I heard anything, and I haven't since I woke up. But it startled me, I guess. I can't go back to sleep again."

"Are you sure you really heard something?"

Tina did not reply for a moment. Then she said, "No.

But I did wake up suddenly. And I got to thinking about you, and decided it was too good a chance to miss."

"I got to agree with you about that. Crawl under the blanket with me, then," Longarm said.

"You're not mad at me for waking you up?" she asked.

"Course not. Why would I be mad?" he asked as Tina snuggled close to him.

"Because I'm so forward," Tina said softly. One of her hands was resting on Longarm's chest and she began moving it up toward his throat.

"There ain't a thing wrong about going after something you want, Tina. Only I ain't the pushy kind."

"Maybe that's one of the things that makes you so interesting. Do you always wait for a woman to make the first move?" As Tina spoke, her hand got busy unbuttoning his balbriggans.

"Mostly I do," Longarm told her. "Like I said, it ain't my way to be pushy."

"Your way might be the best," Tina told him as her fingers reached the last button.

She slid her hand up the ridges of muscle on his abdomen and began stroking his chest, then lowered her head to trace a line of soft quick kisses over his cheeks until her lips reached his mouth. As their lips met Longarm pressed Tina to him and when he felt the tip of her tongue touch his lips he joined his tongue with hers in a clinging kiss.

Tina's full soft breasts were pressing on Longarm's chest. He pulled her to him, and she began turning her torso from side to side, the tips of her budded breasts rasping gently across the mat of curls that covered his chest.

Both of them were breathless now from their long kiss. She sighed as their lips parted and when her gasping ended said, "I don't know about you, but I'm ready for us to start."

Tina straddled him, and Longarm lifted his hips and met her halfway. Tina responded with a throaty cry as her hips descended and fell forward, her lips seeking Longarm's again.

When Tina began shuddering and crying out spasmodically, Longarm brought his hips up and matched her ragged rhythm with quick upward strokes. Tina's cries grew louder and her trembling became a constant jerking twisting. Long-arm gave up trying to match her movements with his upward strokes. He raised his hips and braced his back, letting Tina set her own pace.

Her body stiffened and she shook in a violent, uncon-trollable spasm. Then her body went limp and she collapsed on Longarm, her head falling to his shoulder.

For several minutes Tina did not speak, then she whis-pered into Longarm's ear, "You're the most wonderful lover I've ever known, Longarm. But didn't I do anything for you? You're still as hard and big as when we started."

"We got all night," he told her. "When you get over being tired, we'll start up again."

"But I'm sure not too tired to keep on going, if you want to."

He wrapped his arms around her and rolled them over. Tina sighed as she felt his weight on her and locked her legs around Longarm's hips.

Tina gasped when Longarm lifted himself and drove into her with a sudden lunge, then held himself pressed hard against her.

Longarm relaxed his pressure and lifted his hips. He plunged into her again and she cried out with a throaty whimper, "Do that again!"

Longarm obliged. He lurched down with a fierce thrust that brought another gasp from Tina's throat and then settled down to a fast, steady pace that after a few moments brought her to another trembling frenzy.

Longarm was building to his own climax now, and did not stop his thrusting when Tina shrieked. He held himself back until her body began trembling once more and when her wild cries began for the third time that night he let himself go, drove to completion, then relaxed on her limp form.

"I didn't know what it was like being with a real man," Tina said in a half-whisper.

"You ain't old enough to've been with too many fellows," he said. "And I'd bet they was mostly young bucks."

"I'm nineteen," she told him. "And I've had a few older men, too, but not any of them that gave me the feelings you just did."

Longarm was sleepy now. He stifled a yawn and said, "Let's go to sleep now, Tina. There's tomorrow night, and maybe the next one, too."

"Can I stay with you the rest of the night?" she asked.

"Why, sure. I wouldn't have it any other way."

"Good," she sighed sleepily. "Neither would I."

Tina's words trailed off into silence and her deep rhythmic breathing told Longarm she was asleep. He pulled her closer to him, and let sleep take him, too.

At daybreak Longarm and Tina were on the trail again, crossing the treacherous Settler's Draw. Their quarry had not taken the time to cover his trail, and they had no trouble following him until mid-afternoon, when they had almost reached the opposite side of the broad sink. Then the hoofprints vanished.

"I don't understand it," Tina frowned. "It's like he just stopped here."

"All outlaws knows tricks like that," Longarm told her. "I got a pretty good idea what he done."

"You have?"

"Yep. He put muffles on his horse's feet and led him the rest of the way across. I'd bet a sack of Bull Durham to a box of the best cigars money can buy that he let them muffles stay on till he got outa the draw and a few miles farther on."

"Do you think we can pick up his trail again?"

Longarm shook his head. "Not much of a chance, Tina. About all we can do is turn back."

"And you'll go on to meet that Ranger in Austin?"

"Sure. That's what I come down from Denver to do."

"Will you be back here again?"

"There ain't much way of telling," Longarm replied. "A lot of what I'll be doing depends on what Will Travers tells me when I talk to him in Austin."

"You won't forget me if you do come back, will you?"

"Course not. And, don't forget, we can't make it back to Chiliclothe today. We'll still be camping together tonight."

"I've been thinking about that ever since we started this morning," Tina smiled. "In fact, that's just about all I have been thinking of."

"Well, I ain't exactly forgot it," Longarm replied. "Now, let's admit we was outsmarted and turn around. And don't worry about the Kiowa Kid getting away. He's still on my list, and I ain't a man that gives up easy."

Chapter 8

"I'm right sorry I didn't make it here when I said I would, Will," Longarm said as he shook hands with Will Travers.

"I don't suppose a day or two's going to make that much difference," the Ranger captain replied. "Especially since the Kiowa Kid we've got is still down in the Rio Grande Valley."

"Billy Vail told me you was bringing him here to Austin," Longarm frowned. "What happened to him?"

"It's not as much what happened to him as it is what happened to us," Travers said, not trying to hide his anger. "But it's too hot out here to stay any longer than we have to. I've got a hack waiting outside the depot. Let's finish talking at the Iron Front."

"That'll suit me just fine," Longarm said. "I been nursing what's left of a bottle of Tom Moore, but it's been a long, dry trip and there's not more'n a swallow left."

The air was cool inside the Iron Front Saloon. Travers led Longarm to a table in the back corner, and one of the barkeeps came to get their orders.

"From what you said at the depot, your outfit's got some kind of snarl-up, Will," Longarm said after the barkeep left.

"Oh, it's not my men that're bothering me," Travers replied quickly. "I keep a tight enough rein on them to be sure they won't give me any trouble. It's the damned lawyers that've got me buffaloed."

"Well, now, that ain't exactly new, is it?"

"No. But I think you'll be as put out as I am when I tell you the Kiowa Kid's not here yet. Some jackleg lawyer tied our hands with a writ that keeps us from moving the Kid away from Laredo."

"How come? I always figured your bunch got pretty much what you wanted from the courts in Texas."

"So we do," Travers nodded. "Most of the time."

"Just exactly what'd this lawyer do, Will?"

"He got a court order that keeps us from taking the Kiowa Kid out of Hobbs County. That's where Laredo is."

"I sure never heard of anything like that," Longarm said.

"Nobody else did, far as I can tell. The state attorney said the law was passed right after Reconstruction days, when we got rid of the scallywags from back East that took over Texas after the war was over."

"I can't see why they'd even pass that kind of law."

"Well, it seems that back then the State Police and the Reconstruction scallywags set up a way of arresting anybody they didn't like, and they'd haul 'em here to Austin and tuck 'em away in a jail where nobody could locate 'em."

"Just to keep 'em from making trouble," Longarm nodded.

"That's about the way of it," Travers agreed. "Anyhow, the real Texas people who kicked out the Reconstruction scallywags wanted to make sure nothing like that ever happened again, so they passed this law. Far as I can find out, it never was used until this Laredo lawyer defending the Kiowa Kid dug it up."

"So you're holding the Kid in jail down there but you can't bring him here to try him?"

"That's about the size of it," Travers replied.

"And there's not any way for you to move him?"

"No way we've found so far, and we've sure as hell been looking for one. We've filed two or three writs trying to get him out of jail down there, but the judge has always agreed with that lawyer the Kid hired."

"That ain't too uncommon, Will. I've had a good share of trouble with judges, too." Longarm caught the barkeep's eye and signalled him for a refill. "This round's on me, Will."

"Not likely. You're the guest of the Texas Rangers on this trip," Travers replied.

"Maybe you'll be sorry you invited me after your hear what I got to tell you."

"Bad news?" Travers asked.

"I ain't sure yet."

Travers grunted, then said, "Bad or good, I guess you'd better let me have it."

"That fellow you're holding in Laredo might not be the Kiowa Kid at all," Longarm said.

Travers's expression did not change, nor did he appear to be surprised. He told Longarm, "Well, nobody's perfect, not even us Rangers. But I'd like to know what makes you think we might be holding the wrong man in Laredo."

"Now, that ain't what I said," Longarm answered quickly. "I ain't got any doubts at all that whoever you got in jail down there is guilty of whatever your men pulled him in for. What I was telling you is that maybe he ain't the original Kiowa Kid."

There was no change in Travers's level voice and no worry on his face. He told Longarm, "You ought to know I've thought about that. But the prisoner we're holding in Laredo claims he is, and right now we're willing to take his word for it, because we've got a plan to get our hands on him, with your help."

"Damn it, Will! You're acting just like Billy Vail now!" Longarm exclaimed. "When he told me you had the Kiowa Kid down here in Texas, I spent a long time trying to show him that you and your outfit might've arrested the wrong man!"

"I just got through telling you that I've already thought

that might be the case," Travers replied. "Billy Vail's already told me you're convinced that an outlaw buried up in the Nation was the Kiowa Kid," Travers said quietly. "Then Billy said that after that one you came off best in a shootout with another Kiowa Kid up in Dakota Territory. From what Billy told me, you watched him being buried."

"That's right!" Longarm broke in. "And after that train I was coming here on broke down, I had a brush with *another* Kiowa Kid up on the Red River."

Travers frowned. "The hell you did! I haven't heard about that. Was it on the Texas side of the Red or over in Indian Territory?"

"It was in Texas, all right. Little jerkwater town called Chilicothe."

"I know where it is," Travers said. "Go on, tell me what happened."

Longarm took time to light a fresh cheroot before he went on, "I sent you a wire about the train breakdown, so you'd know about that. Well, me and the fireman started for a track crew shanty a couple of miles down the track and somebody tried to bushwhack us. Neither one of us seen him, and we didn't have horses to chase him with, so after I'd swapped a shot or two with the bushwhacker, me and the railroader went on to Chilicothe. When we got there, the night marshal had been killed, and before he died he claimed it was the Kiowa Kid."

"I suppose the marshal had run into the Kid somewhere else?" Travers broke in to ask.

"He claimed he had. He's supposed to've known him someplace over in Arizona."

"So you took out after the killer?"

"Why, sure. Borrowed a horse in Chilicothe and picked up his trail maybe six hours after he'd tried to kill me and that railroad man."

"I suppose the Kid was heading for Indian Territory?"

"He had to be. I guess he got there, too, because he had so much of a start I didn't have a chance to catch up with him."

"You didn't even see him, then?"

"Oh, I got a glimpse of him when he was trying to bushwhack us, but he was galloping away hell for leather. Anyhow, what I'm getting at, Will, is that with this fellow that popped up there in Chilicothe, and the two that I run into before, that's three Kiowa Kids. The one you got down in Laredo makes four, and that's just too damn many."

"Well, I'll admit it does strain a man's belief in folks' eyesight," Travers agreed. "And I don't see any way to prove that the fellow we've got in jail is the real Kiowa Kid, any more than you can prove he's the one you have your dust-up with on the way down here."

"Or whether either one of the two I seen buried was the real one," Longarm added.

Travers said, "That, too. Well, I'm right sorry I dragged you down here for nothing, Longarm. When I talked with Billy in Denver, I was dead sure we had the real Kid, but I had a little bit more than that to talk about, too. Why don't we go over to headquarters, and I'll tell you what I had in mind when I stopped off to see Billy on my way home."

Headquarters of the Texas Rangers was a ramshackle frame house that stood in one corner of a large clear space near the center of Austin. Travers's office was a corner room at the back of the building. It was furnished with a rolltop desk, three or four chairs, and an oak file cabinet.

"Have a seat," the Ranger invited. "I'll go get Sergeant Carter. He's in charge of the Kiowa Kid case."

"No need to go looking for me, Will," said a man who came in the door before Travers could turn. "I saw you come in."

"Sit down and join us, then," Travers told him. "And shake hands with Deputy U. S. Marshal Custis Long."

"Glad to make your acquaintance, Marshal Long," Carter said. "I've sure heard a lot about you."

"Same to you, Sergeant," Longarm replied. "But most of the folks I know call me Longarm, like Will does."

"You know why Longarm's here, Frank," Travers went on.

"Sure," Carter nodded. "But before we start talking about

70

this damn case, I'd better tell you that it might not be the Kiowa Kid we've got in jail down in Laredo. While you were at the depot, we got a wire from the sheriff up in Montague County. He says two men held up the Fort Worth & Denver train this morning just outside of Bowie and robbed the passengers and mail car. They killed the postal clerk in the mail car and got away with two sacks of registered mail and whatever money there was in the mail-car safe."

"Wait a minute!" Longarm exclaimed. "Seems to me I seen that name Bowie on one of the stations just a little ways south of Chilicothe, Will. Am I right, or was I dreaming?"

"No, you passed through Bowie on the way here," Travers assured him.

"Then that fellow that was potshooting at me and the railroad man the other day could've been the same one I was chasing."

"It's an odds-on bet you're right," the Ranger captain nodded. "I imagine he went to meet his partner in Indian Territory and then both of them headed for Bowie." Turning back to Carter, he asked, "Did that sheriff want us to help him run the robbers down?"

Carter shook his head. "No. Him and his deputy was going after the outlaws. But I was pretty sure you'd want to know about the robbery, because one of the holdup men bragged to the passengers that he was the Kiowa Kid."

"God almighty, Will!" Longarm exploded. "I'm starting to think there's really another Kiowa Kid around, or one of them I seen buried has rose up outa his grave!"

"I'd say that's about the point I've reached, too, by now," Travers replied. "Did the sheriff say anything more, Frank?"

"Not a helluva lot. I thought Marshal Long might be interested, though. Since the train robbers took two mail sacks, it's a federal case."

"Billy Vail ain't likely to send a man out on it unless the sheriff asks for help," Longarm volunteered.

"Even if one of the robbers might turn out to be the Kiowa Kid?" Travers asked.

"I reckon that might stir Billy up a little bit," Longarm nodded thoughtfully. "But we got a pretty full platter, and he keeps bellyaching about not having enough deputies. Course, he might put somebody on it, seeing as how the Kiowa Kid is supposed to be one of them holdup men."

"If he does, I expect you'll be getting a wire from him pretty soon," Travers said. "And he knows how to get hold of you if he decides to change cases on you."

Carter asked Longarm, "You'll be around the office for a while, I guess, in case we get a wire from your chief?"

"Sure," Longarm nodded. "I don't suppose this new holdup changes anything you got in mind, does it, Will?"

"Not a bit," Travers assured him as Carter left.

"Go ahead and lay it out for me," Longarm suggested.

"I've had to make a few changes in the plan that Billy and I talked about in Denver," Travers began. "Billy asked me if we knew of any crimes he'd committed that might come under federal jurisdiction."

"Hold up a minute, Will," Longarm interrupted. "Maybe I can save you some breath. You was going to have Billy send me down here to take a look at the Kiowa Kid you're holding and see if I can identify him, and find out if he's wanted on a federal warrant, so I can get him outa the Laredo jail if he is."

"A federal warrant would have to be honored, Longarm," Travers pointed out. "You could go down to Laredo and serve it, and they'd have to turn the Kid over to you."

"Then I guess you and Billy will figure out a way for you Rangers to get him back. Am I right?"

"That's how our scheme started out," Travers said.

"But now there's another Kiowa Kid on the loose," Longarm went on thoughtfully. "The one that killed the postal clerk when he held up that mail car up in Bowie. So now we got a Kiowa Kid that's got to be brought in for sure on a federal charge, and that's upset your applecart."

"Right again," the Ranger captain agreed.

"Damned if you ain't got apples rolling loose all over the state of Texas, Will!" Longarm exclaimed. "And you're looking to me to gather 'em up for you."

"I suppose you could put it that way."

Longarm took a cheroot from his pocket and made a long business of lighting it. He said slowly, "You know how I feel about crooks and outlaws, Will. Was it up to me, I'd change the law around so that any outlaw that had more'n one crime on his record would take his last walk up the steps of a gallows."

"I feel the same way sometime, especially when they get freed because of some lawyers' tricks," Travers said.

"I guess you could say we both respect the law, Will, but neither one of us has got much use for lawyers that twist the law around to help a crook," Longarm told the Ranger. "Except I can't bring myself to lie about anybody, even if he's an outlaw. I might shave pretty close to the line sometimes, but so far I ain't had to step over it."

"Are you telling me yes or no?" Travers asked.

"Neither one, right this minute. I ain't so sure this scheme you and Billy figured out would work, and I ain't so sure I could take it on without having to lie about what we was doing."

"Billy told me that was about what you'd say," Travers nodded. "That's why he sent you down here to listen to my side of the story. But it looks like he was right about that conscience of yours."

"Well, I ain't said no yet," Longarm said slowly. "Maybe there's some kinda twist you and Billy missed seeing that'd make your scheme work out."

"Suppose you stick around here in Austin for a day or so," Travers suggested. "You can do your thinking here as well as you can in Denver, I guess."

Before Longarm could reply, Sergeant Carter came hurrying into Travers's office carrying two sheets of yellow flimsy. "These two wires just got here, Will," he said. "One of them's for you, from the chief of police at Laredo. The other one's for Marshal Long from his chief."

Longarm and Travers took the telegrams and read them. Will Travers finished his first. "It looks like you'll have to do your thinking on the train, Longarm. I've got to get to Laredo in a hurry. The Kiowa Kid's just escaped from jail."

Longarm replied, "I ain't sure how much time I'm going to have for thinking in the next few days, Will. Billy's sending me to handle that mail robbery up at Bowie. He wants me up there right away."

Chapter 9

For a moment, Longarm and Travers stared at one another. Then Travers said, "It looks like we'll have to put off trying to get the Kiowa Kid up here to Austin."

"Well, that don't mean we can't get back to it again, soon as I take care of this new case," Longarm pointed out.

"Sure," Travers nodded. "It makes sense for you to take on that mail robbery. Chances are the outlaws headed right over the Red River for the Indian Nation, and your badge is good there. Once any of us Rangers get outside of Texas, our badges don't have any legal standing."

"It won't hurt if we just let things stand the way they are for a little while," Longarm said.

"I suppose not," Travers agreed. "When I get down to Laredo and catch up with our Kiowa Kid again, or bring him back dead, I'll send Billy a wire. Now, is there anything we can do to help you get ready to go?"

"Not a thing, Will. I ain't had time to rent a hotel room, so I won't have to pack. All I need to do is find out when the next train's pulling out for Bowie."

Before Travers could answer, Carter said, "There's an I&GN passenger haul leaving for Fort Worth in about an hour. It makes connections there with the night Fort Worth & Denver train, and if both of them run on time you'll be in Bowie around midnight. You can almost always find a hack in front of the Congress building, and it's just a short walk from here, right across the square."

"Thanks, Sergeant," Longarm nodded. He shook hands with Carter and Travers, slid his arms into the sleeves of his coat, and donned his hat. Picking up his rifle and valise, he told Travers, "You know, maybe this is a lucky case for both of us, Will. If we luck out and close both our cases, we won't have to wade up to our bellybuttons in Kiowa Kids no more."

Longarm stepped off the train in Bowie a little before midnight. In spite of the late hour, the little town was still busy.

About half the stores were dark, their doors closed and their windows shuttered, but those that remained open did not lack customers. Far down the street he could see light shining through a barred window, which identified the building as the sheriff's office and jail. He could count the saloons by the light that showed at the tops and bottoms of their batwings; five of them stood along the street. There were men gathered in front of all of them, but the biggest crowd, a dozen or more, was at the saloon almost directly across from the depot.

Its lights were brighter than most of the others, and its front was higher. There were windows just below the roofline, indicating rooms on the second floor. A pair of Pintsch carbide lanterns hung from the eaves near the peak of the high gabled roof and illuminated a sign on the high false front: LADY MAY.

Longarm headed for it. The men around the door opened a lane to let him pass and he pushed through the batwings. To his surprise, the cavernous barroom was almost empty. All the tables were deserted and only four customers stood at the bar, two pairs of men standing talking, their heads close together.

As he walked slowly to the deserted rear section of the bar Longarm looked around for a barkeep, but saw none. He stopped a few feet from the back wall, dropped his valise to the floor, and leaned his Winchester across it. As he straightened up, a door in the rear wall opened and a woman came through it.

Her hair was brassy blonde and she wore it in high-piled curls. Her eyes shone blue below thin pencilled brows, and her full lips were carefully outlined with rouge. She wore a saloon girl's abbreviated dress, salmon-red and trimmed with gold braid, the hemline barely to here knees, the bodice cut low and fitted tightly.

She was carrying an armful of bottles, and she stopped at the end of the mahogany to unload them. The bottles began to slip from her arms and Longarm saw what was about to happen. He took a long, quick step to her side and grabbed the slippery bottles before they could fall to the floor.

"Thanks, mister," she said. "What whiskey costs these days is sinful. You saved me a handful of cash, and I owe you. Your first drink's on the house."

"Well, that's right nice of you," he said. "And a drink's what I come in for."

"What'll it be, then?" she asked.

"If you got some good Maryland rye, maybe a bottle of Tom Moore, that'd be my choice."

"Well, glory be!" she exclaimed. "A rye man! Mister, I'll not only pour you a glass of Tom Moore, I'll have one with you myself."

Pouring generous shots into the glasses, she pushed one to him, picked up the other, and held it out for Longarm to clink his glass against it.

Longarm swallowed half the pungent rye, put his glass back on the bar, and lighted a cheroot. She was, he told himself, quite some bundle of woman, and there was a certain manner about her that seemed to set her apart from the usual saloon girl. By the time he had his cigar drawing well he had made his decision.

"For all the people that's out on the street, it looks to

me like you got a slow night here," he said.

"And I'm glad it is," she replied. "I'm without my regular barkeep. Generally, I don't tend bar, I just walk around and make the customers feel welcome."

Longarm suspected that her duties extended to a bit more than that, but he did not comment.

"Those men who're hanging around outside don't amount to much," she went on. "They're the town riffraff. Most of the able-bodied men are out with a sheriff's posse, trying to run down a couple of outlaws that held up a train here yesterday and killed one of the crew."

"I sorta suspicioned that might be the way of it," Longarm nodded. "That train robbery's what's brought me to Bowie."

"Is that right?" she asked. "What are you, a lawman?"

"My name's Long, ma'am, Custis Long. I'm a deputy U. S. marshal outa the Denver office."

"Denver? And you've come all the way here to help the sheriff catch those outlaws?"

"That's about the size of it," he nodded. "And, even if it ain't exactly a secret, I'll appreciate it if you don't make a lot of talk about me being here."

"Well, sure, if that's what you want. You sure could've fooled me about your job, though. I had you figured to be a rancher. I guess they sent you instead of a Ranger?"

"You might say that, I guess," Longarm nodded. "Fact of the matter is, I happened to be down in Austin, and my chief wired me to get up here fast instead of him having to send a man all the way from Denver."

"It's too bad you got here too late to join the posse," she said. "This is only Sheriff Becker's first term in office, and I imagine he could use some help. They say one of the outlaws is a real bad one called the Kiowa Kid."

"So I heard," Longarm replied. He sipped his drink and went on, "I don't suppose you'd have any idea where that posse might be? Or when it'll be back?"

"They could be anyplace by now," she said. "Maybe even on the way back. Sheriff Becker said the robbers might've headed for Indian Territory. It's only about twenty miles away. When he was gathering up the posse he told the men that if the outlaws got across the river they'd have to turn back."

"I sure can't track 'em in the dark," Longarm observed. "I guess the best thing I can do is wait for 'em here. I seen your upstairs rooms was all dark when I rode up. You think I can rent one for the rest of the night?"

"Well, Marshal, this a saloon, not a rooming house," she said slowly. "These rooms are for the help here. And we haven't got a hotel in Bowie yet."

"Now, if renting a room to me would get you in trouble with your boss, don't bother," Longarm told her. "I can just ease down and catch forty winks in one of them chairs over there while I'm waiting. I've slept in a lot worse places."

"I haven't said no," she said quickly. "We've got a room vacant upstairs because we're shorthanded, and you're welcome to use it rent-free, Marshal Long."

"But what's your boss going to say?"

"Not one word. You see, I happen to be the boss. I guess you didn't notice the sign on the outside."

"You mean the Lady May belongs to you?"

"It certainly does," she said. "Ask anybody in Montague County who the Lady May belongs to and they'll tell you Maybelle Morgan. That's me."

"I guess I just taken too much for granted," he told her. "But it didn't occur to me you might be—" Longarm stopped.

"Anything but a saloon girl? I've passed through that stage, Marshal. Now, would you like another drink before you go up to bed? It's still on the house."

"Thanks, no, Miz Morgan. I'm tireder than I am thirsty."

"It's just May, Marshal Long. And I know how it feels to be tired and draggy after a train ride."

"I reckon. And I do thank you for letting me bunk down for a while."

"No thanks needed. I can't go up there with you, because I'm the only one here; the night barkeep's not due for another hour or so," May said. "But the room's at the front on the right of the stairs, and the door's unlocked. There's a key inside. Get a good sleep now."

"I sure aim to," Longarm replied.

Longarm had no idea how long he'd been sleeping, but the edge had been taken off his fatigue when the faint metallic grating of metal against metal wakened him.

As always, he was alert the instant his eyes opened. The light from the Pintsch lanterns made the room seem bright. He lifted his Colt from the chair and held it ready. The metallic scraping ended with a click. The doorknob turned and the door swung slowly open.

Swivelling his Colt to cover the door, Longarm said in a calm voice, "Whoever you are, you better come in with your hands up. I got a Colt in my hand and I know how to use it."

"I'm sure you do, Marshal Long," May Morgan's voice replied.

She stepped into the room and Longarm saw that she wore only a clinging negligee and carried a bottle in one hand. In her other hand was a "landlord's friend," a metal tube with a slot on one end and a handle on the other, a device used to open ward-locks in hotels and boarding houses.

"If you want me to go back to my own room, I will," she went on. "But I thought you might like another drink of Tom Moore, so I brought a bottle with me."

"Miz Morgan!" Longarm said. He lowered the Colt. "I sure wasn't expecting to have your company, or anybody else's, come to that."

"You don't mind if I come in, do you?" she asked.

"Now, it'd be real impolite of me to say no to a lady that was good-hearted enough to put me up for the night," Longarm told her. "And I don't ever remember a time when I turned down a drink of Maryland rye."

"That's what I was hoping you'd say, Marshal Long," May smiled. She put the bottle on the bureau and Longarm saw the cork had been half-pulled. After she'd removed the cork, she held out the bottle and went on, "Since you're my guest, it's only polite for me to offer you the first drink."

"I don't mind if I do," he said. Then, as she handed him the bottle, he added, "But I got a sorta nickname my friends call me by. It's Longarm."

"Of course," May chuckled, sitting on the bed beside Longarm as he took a healthy swig of the pungent rye. "The long arm of the law."

"Something like that," he agreed, handing her the bottle. May tilted the Tom Moore and swallowed once, then again. She closed her eyes for a moment, then opened them and fixed them on Longarm. "You know, Longarm, I couldn't make up my mind for quite a while whether I ought to disturb your rest. But when we were talking downstairs, I got the idea you're a man who understands women, so I decided it'd be all right."

"Well, I wouldn't exactly say I understand women," Longarm protested mildly. "But I got to admit I enjoy their company."

"And it doesn't surprise you when a woman takes the first step toward a man who attracts her," she went on.

As May spoke, she laid her hand on Longarm's knee and slid it slowly up to his crotch. She let her hand lie motionless until she felt him begin to stiffen in response to the warm pressure of her palm, then slipped her hand inside his underwear and closed it around his semi-erection. With her free hand she started to unbutton his longjohns.

Longarm slid May's robe off her plump white shoulders and she shrugged to let the filmy garment slip free. Her breasts were as he'd imagined they'd be, bulging globes just a bit too large for her build, with creamy-smooth skin and large pink pebbled rosettes.

Bending down, Longarm took one of the rosettes into his mouth and began caressing it with his tongue. May quivered and gasped.

"You sure know how to please a woman," she whispered, her voice a bit uneven.

Bracing his legs, Longarm lifted May bodily and lowered her to the bed. May sprawled her milk-white thighs.

Longarm swung himself around. He felt May's hands on his shaft, positioning him, and drove into her with a long, sustained plunge. May began bucking her hips frantically.

As Longarm settled down to a long steady stroking, May's upward bucks to meet him grew more and more frantic.

Suddenly she screamed and started shuddering convulsively. Longarm slowed his rhythm until her shivering faded and her screams became long throaty sighs, but he still kept driving into her.

Longarm kept up his long steady thrusts until May began gasping and wriggling once more. When her hips started rising to meet his lunges he speeded up. May locked her legs around his back, pulling herself upward as he ended his downward lunges, until he felt her beginning to quiver.

Longarm was almost ready. He drove faster as his own time for a climax came closer, and by this time May was bucking again. Longarm pounded on as her sharp cries rose in the night. When he felt her going into her final convulsive spasms he lunged with a few final finishing drives until he jetted and sighed happily and let himself go limp, dropping to rest on her soft, quivering body.

May sighed as Longarm rolled off to stretch out beside her. "It's just about the best feeling I've ever had."

"You do a man good, May," Longarm said. "We'll rest a while, maybe have a nap, then just see what happens."

"I don't think either one of us has to guess about that," she told him. "All I can say is, I hope the sheriff and his posse don't get back here until next week."

Chapter 10

Loud voices and hoofbeats roused Longarm from his exhausted sleep. The room was bright, and he realized that daylight had arrived while he slept. Glancing around, he saw that May had gone.

Longarm rose and padded across the room in his bare feet. Pulling back one of the shades, he looked down. The sheriff's posse had just returned. A crowd was forming. There were already fifteen or twenty men milling around several riders who had pulled up in front of the saloon. Everybody in the crowd seemed to be talking at the same time.

Turning away from the window, Longarm saw the bottle of Tom Moore standing on the dresser, his balbriggans folded neatly beside it. When he got to the dresser and reached for the bottle he noticed a scrap of paper resting on the longjohns and bent down to read the few words scrawled on the scrap.

"Thanks, Longarm. We'll finish the bottle tonight."

With a smile, Longarm uncorked the rye and tilted it to his lips. He picked up his underwear and went back to the bed. Sitting down, he lighted a cheroot and puffed it while dressing.

By the time Longarm had dressed and gone downstairs the posse and the crowd had moved from the street into the Lady May. Longarm stopped in the doorway for a moment, trying to identify the sheriff in the shifting crowd. He caught a glimpse of a badge flashing on the vest of a tall, wiry man.

"You'd be Sheriff Becker, I guess?" Longarm asked.

"Sure am." Becker's eyes were measuring Longarm as he replied. "What's on your mind?"

"About the same thing that's on yours, I'd imagine," Longarm replied. He took his wallet out and flipped it open to show Becker his badge. "I'm Custis Long, Sheriff, outa the Denver office. My chief sent me down here to be whatever help I can on this train-robbery case."

"You're a mite late getting here, I'd say," Becker said. "I know the U. S. marshal's office has got jurisdiction, because the mail coach was robbed and the clerk killed, and I was looking for somebody to get here sooner."

"Well, better late than never," Longarm told Becker. "I don't guess your posse run across the outlaws?"

Becker snorted. "Hell, no! Not after the start they had!"

"I figured you hadn't, or that'd've been the first thing you told me," Longarm said.

By now the men in the saloon were pushing to get closer so they could hear better. Realizing anything he and the sheriff said would be circulating as gossip almost at once, Longarm decided he needed privacy before going on.

"Maybe we better go down to your office before we talk any more, Sheriff," he suggested.

"Why, sure," Becker agreed.

Outside the saloon, Sheriff Becker pulled the reins of his horse free of the hitch rail and led the tired animal. He and Longarm walked shoulder to shoulder.

"Go ahead and ask your questions, Marshal Long," Becker said. "But I don't expect I know much that'll help."

"You'd sure know more than I do," Longarm pointed out. "I was about five or six hundred miles away when it happened, and you was right here."

"I hadn't quite looked at it that way," Becker said.

"And I hope you don't feel like I'm butting in and pushing you to one side in your own jurisdiction," Longarm went on.

Becker shook his head. "Not a bit of it, Marshal Long." He paused, frowned, and went on, "Long? You wouldn't be the one that's called Longarm, would you?"

"Far as I know, there ain't another one with my name on the marshal's roster."

"Why sure! I never have run into you, but I've sure heard folks talk about you."

They reached the sheriff's office. Becker unlocked the door and swung it open, gesturing for Longarm to enter. He sat down beside the battered rolltop desk while Becker hung up his hat and settled down in his slightly lopsided swivel chair.

"Now, go ahead and ask your questions," he told Longarm. "I'll do my best to give you straight answers."

"Let's start off at the beginning," Longarm suggested. "If you'll just tell me how the robbers worked, it'll help a lot."

"I figure they were old hands that knew just what to do," Becker began. "They worked their job right slick. Stopped the train with a red flag just as the locomotive got close to the end of a long trestle, then uncoupled it and made the engineer pull ahead and stop."

Longarm nodded. "I see what the holdup men had in mind. The passengers was sorta marooned out on that trestle, I'd imagine."

"They sure were," Becker agreed. "Then the robbers pulled the safety plug on the engine cylinders so it lost all its steam, and after they'd tied up the engineer and the fireman, they went back down the trestle to the cars and made the passengers hand over what they had before they took on the mail coach."

"That's when they killed the mail clerk, I suppose?"

Nodding, Becker went on, "He'd locked the mail-coach doors and was holed up inside with a sawed-off twelve-gauge. The robbers split up, one at each end of the coach. They broke out the glass in the doors with their gun-butts at the same time, which put the clerk in a crossfire. I don't guess there'd be any way to tell which one killed him."

"It don't matter," Longarm put in. "The law says they're both guilty."

Becker nodded. "Well, after they got into the car I don't suppose it was much of a job for them to empty the safe—shot off the knob and punched out the lock—then they made their getaway. Oh, it was a smooth job, all right. They must've been old-timers who knew exactly what they wanted to do."

"Is that why you figure the Kiowa Kid was one of them?" Longarm asked. "You'd heard the Kiowa Kid had just pulled a job up around Chilicothe?"

"Well, the Fort Worth & Denver station agent here in town had told me the Kiowa Kid had been in some kind of scrape up the line at Chilicothe a couple of days before," Becker replied. "So I decided that it was him. This job here was so slick, and the Kiowa Kid was in the neighborhood."

"When you searched around the trestle, did you find anything?" Longarm asked. "Any kind of evidence at all?"

Becker's face went blank for a moment, then he shook his head and said, "Damned if I didn't forget all about searching. It was still raining pretty good when I got out there, and after I'd snaked back and forth along that trestle a few times, I was soaked. Once the engine got up steam and started off, all that I had in mind was heading for home."

"You must've got a description of the robbers from the passengers and train crew," Longarm said. "And someplace they must've said something about one of them fellows that put you in mind of the Kiowa Kid."

"Now, that's one funny thing I haven't come to yet," the sheriff replied. "Both of those outlaws were dressed just alike. Both of 'em had on brown hats and yellow range slickers and red bandana masks that just showed their eyes between their hatbrims and the top of the bandanas."

Longarm puffed hard on his cheroot while he held his temper in check. He got angry every time he thought of the stupidity of a political system that allowed a totally inexperienced man to hold a sheriff's job.

As the smoke swirled away, he asked Becker, "And you still figured one of 'em was the Kiowa Kid, even without knowing what either one looked like?"

"I guess that was a fool thing to do, wasn't it?" Becker said. "But just the same, he was spotted up in Chilicothe just a few days before, and he'd had plenty of time to get here."

"That's true enough," Longarm agreed. He didn't make Becker feel worse by telling him about his own experiences in Chilicothe, but asked, "How far is it to the place where that train was held up?"

"Oh, two and a half miles, not quite three."

"Tell you what, Sheriff Becker," Longarm went on, "let's me and you take a ride out to that trestle and see if we can't find something."

"Why, sure," Becker agreed. "We can go back to the Lady May and I'll get you a horse from one of my possemen so we won't have to fool around at the livery stable waiting for Sim to saddle one up."

Within five minutes, Longarm and the sheriff were riding beside the railroad right-of-way. Like almost all trackage on Western railroads, there was only one set of rails after they left the depot sidings, and only the lowest humps in the rolling ground had been trenched and the shallowest depressions filled to level the tracks.

After they had covered perhaps half the distance, the terrain grew rougher. Small gullies cut the land at short intervals and many of these had been too deep to fill, but were spanned by short trestles. After they had been riding for a quarter of an hour or so across the cut-up country, the sheriff pointed to a spot ahead where the rails disappeared into a steep-sided manmade cut.

"That's where the real rough country starts," he told Longarm. "The trestle where the robbers stoped the train is at the bottom of that cut. Goes over a right deep canyon where a river must've run once. The canyon's about a mile wide, but you don't see the trestle till you're almost right up to it because it runs slantwise across the canyon."

"Which means the tracks curves there, and a train would be moving mightly slow, going downgrade into it," Longarm said.

"You're either a good guesser or you know a lot about railroads, Longarm," Becker said.

"Well, I've rode on trains a lot and I've done a lot of guessing, but I don't take no special credit for either one."

"Just the same, you're right. It doesn't make much difference which way a train's going, it just about has to make a full stop at this end of the cut."

They had reached the beginning of the cut by now. Becker reined his horse over between the rails. Longarm followed suit, and the horses moved even more slowly as they started down the grade. Longarm saw at a glance that Becker's description of the terrain had been accurate. It was an ideal place for a holdup. Longarm studied the terrain a moment, then turned to his companion. "I take it the train was coming across the trestle heading toward this side, and outlaws was waiting down below, at the end of the trestle?"

"Yes," Becker nodded. "And they made their getaway out of this end, too."

"Then their horses must've been hid someplace close to the tracks. We ought've passed it a little ways back," Longarm explained. "When you found the place where they were tethered, did you run across anything they might've dropped?"

"Why, we—" Becker began, then shook his head. "I won't try to shade the facts, Longarm. I was so anxious to start out after the holdup men that I didn't look around to see where they'd hidden their mounts. Now that I think about it, they wouldn't've had to hide their horses at all. The train was moving this way, and they'd've gotten out of sight by the time any of the train crew or passengers could've gotten up here and seen them."

In spite of the steep grade down which they were moving, Longarm reined in. Becker stopped with him.

"What's the matter?" the sheriff asked.

"Nothing, except I don't think we need to go all the way

down there. At least not now," Longarm said. "Let's just set here a minute while I get the lay of the land in my head and ask you a question or two."

"Ask away," Becker nodded.

"When you got here, where was the engine and the cars?"

"Like I told you, the coaches were just past the middle of the trestle. The engine was right at this end of it."

"Did the engineer tell you when he seen the robbers?"

"He said he didn't see them until they jumped on the engine steps right behind the cab. One was on his side, the other on the fireman's side. And both of them had guns in their hands."

"You know what that makes me think?" Longarm asked. When Becker shook his head, he went on, "It's real likely them two robbers worked for a railroad sometime or other. A man'd have to know his business pretty well to be sure he could jump at just exactly the right time to land where they did."

"I suppose that's right." Becker nodded thoughtfully.

"And they'd have to know beforehand just where they had to be to leave them coaches where the passengers would have the most trouble trying to take after them. Or shoot 'em, if any of the passengers had guns, which is pretty likely.

"And they'd have to know how to put the safety valves outa whack so the steam would rush out," Longarm went on. "Was I you, I'd've looked for any men in Bowie that was real close friends and used to work for a railroad, before I got up a posse and begun riding all over hell's half-acre."

"Everything you've said sounds sensible," Becker admitted.

"I think it does," Longarm agreed, his voice gentle. "I reckon we've seen enough here. Let's scramble up to the top of this cut again and take a look-see over the land."

"You mind telling me what we are looking for?" Becker asked as he and Longarm reached the top of the steep grade.

Before he answered, Longarm reined in, and Becker also brought his horse to a halt.

"I ain't real sure," Longarm said. "I just got a hunch

them crooks might've been in such a hurry to put this place behind 'em that they left something that'd help make a case against 'em."

"What kind of something?"

"Damned if I know," Longarm told him. "But I've found that when somebody's running away from a crime they're generally in an awful hurry, and when a man's in a rush he gets careless."

Rising in his stirrups, Longarm began scanning the terrain. Becker did not stand up, but he also began looking at the broken prairie that stretched out below them.

"If you was going to hide a horse anyplace close by, where'd you be most likely to tether it, sheriff?" Longarm asked.

Becker hesitated for a moment, then pointed to a rock outcrop fifty yards or so from the bottom of the rise the railroad cut ran through. "I'd say right there. It's close, and the ground around it's fairly smooth. You could get to it fast, and your horse would have firm ground to start from."

"You got a good eye," Longarm nodded. "Let's just go take a look."

They half-rode, half-skidded their mounts down the incline and reined them to the spot Becker had indicated. After he had studied the area for a moment, Longarm pointed and asked Becker, "Don't that patch right at the base of them high rocks look a mite funny to you?"

His eyes following Longarm's pointing finger, the sheriff replied, "It does, at that. Looks like the rocks around the base of that middle outcrop have been disturbed."

"They might've been," Longarm said. "Let's go look."

As their horses drew closer to the outcrop, it was easy to see signs of recent digging at its base. There were changes in color at the base of a few larger rocks, indicating that until very recently they had been imbedded in the soil deeper than they were now. When they reined in, Longarm and Becker did not need to discuss the signs. They dismounted at once and walked over to the outcrop.

"Somebody moved those three big rocks not too long

ago," Becker said, pointing to the stone formation. "Look how loose that dirt is."

They began digging with their hands, removing the loose dirt. Within a few minutes they could overturn the larger stones and shove them aside. Shifting the third rock uncovered a strip of bright yellow fabric, and they shifted the stones around it until they could pull out a pair of yellow oiled silk slickers, the standard rain garb of most cowhands.

"Well, Sheriff," Longarm said, "looks like them robbers got rid of these first thing after they'd done their job."

"They must have," Becker said. "But I don't see anything special about them that'd help us find who they belonged to. Nine out of ten cowpunchers around here own a slicker just like these. Hell, I've got one myself."

"I grant you that," Longarm said. "Except these look like they're brand-new. How many cowhands you know that'd bury a brand-new slicker?"

"You think they were bought for this holdup, then?"

"I figure it's likely. And maybe we don't know how to look at 'em right. Ain't there a store in Bowie that sells them?"

"Sure. Dade's General Merchandise has slickers like these, and so does the other big store, Goldenson's."

"They'd be likely to know more about 'em than we do," Longarm said. "Let's get on back to town and find out."

Chapter 11

"We'll get to Goldenson's store first," Becker said as he and Longarm reached the first houses on their return to Bowie. "But I still don't see what good we're doing. This kind of slicker's common as dirt; you'll find 'em everyplace you look."

"We got to make a stab at it, just the same," Longarm replied.

When they showed the slickers to Goldenson, the store-keeper took one look at them and shook his head. "I don't sell this make of slicker, gentlemen," he said, pointing to a rack across the aisle on which a dozen yellow slickers hung.

To Longarm they looked alike, but Goldenson went on, "I buy my stock from Simpson in New York. If you look closely at those on the rack there, you'll see they have flannel collar insets. These two you have use canvas insets; they're made by Federal in Chicago. Dade's carries their line."

At Dade's, Longarm and Becker had better luck. Dade

glanced at he slickers and nodded. "That's the kind I carry, all right."

"Question is, did you sell these two?" Longarm said.

"I can tell you in about ten seconds," Dade replied. "Let me take a closer look." He turned the collar up at the back of the neck, glanced at it, and nodded. "Yes, I sold this one." A similar quick look at the second brought an identical response. "This one, too."

"You mind telling us how you knew that so fast?" Longarm asked. "And whether you're absolutely sure?"

"Not a bit, provided you don't pass the word on to my customers," Dade replied.

Becker said quickly, "It's not for public use, Mort."

"Unless you get called on to testify about it in court," Longarm added.

"You mean these are evidence in some kind of crime?" the storekeeper asked.

"We can't tell yet," Becker replied. "We're trying to get a line on who the slickers belong to."

"That train robbery the other day?" When the sheriff nodded, the storekeeper went on, "I can identify them as having been sold in my store by the price that I put on my merchandise in a little code."

Longarm picked up one of the slickers and turned up the back collar flap, as he'd seen the storekeeper do. Showing in sharp black lines against the yellow fabric were three letters, O-T-A.

"I guess you mean these three letters?" he asked Dade.

"Yes. That's a code a lot of storekeepers use. It's very easy to read after you get used to it."

"You mind explaining it to me and the sheriff? It ain't something we're likely to talk about."

"My code word is 'cowpasture,'" Dade explained. "Any ten-letter word in which no letter is repeated can be used, of course. And it's simple letter for number substitution: C means one, O means two, W is three, and so down to E, which is zero." When Longarm began counting on his fingers, Dade went on, "I'll save you the trouble, Marshal Long. That slicker cost me $2.75 wholesale."

"But you got to sell it for more to make a profit," Longarm said. "So you add your profit on top of that. What I don't see is why you go to the trouble of writing down what you paid for a thing. Seems to me it'd be easier to just put on what you sell it for."

"Oh, I put that on a tag, right on the merchandise," Dade said. "But I can see you don't know much about storekeeping, Marshal Long. Most customers like to dicker me down to a lower price. Now, I can't remember what I paid for every item I've got in stock, and my clerks don't always know the wholesale price of what they're selling. Whether it's me or a clerk who's dickering with a customer, we can't take time to go look at my account books. So I put the cost price on the merchandise."

"Now I get it," Longarm said. "You can see right off how much you paid for something. Then you'll know how much you can let 'em dicker you down and still make some money."

"That's about the size of it," Dade nodded. "But I remember these slickers. They've got a few crooked seams, so I got a real good price on them from the manufacturer. I ordered a big lot, because I could undersell Goldenson on them, and I sold the last of them just a few weeks ago. The new ones cost me a dollar more apiece."

"Do you remember who bought them?" Becker asked quickly.

"Certainly. You see, I'd sold all but two of that bunch of slickers, and I cut the price for those last two way below what I usually charge."

"Who bought them, then?" Becker asked.

"Why, the Boyd brothers."

"Jeff and Joe Boyd?" Becker asked. "The ones that run that little vest-pocket spread about eight miles south of town?"

The storekeeper nodded. "They each wanted a slicker, so I cut my price way down for them."

"Would you be willing to get up and swear to that in court, Mr. Dade?" Longarm asked quickly.

"Why, yes, I guess I would," Dade answered. "You mean

it was Jeff and Joe Boyd who robbed that train the other day?"

"It sure looks like it," Becker said.

Longarm put in, "I don't guess we need to ask you not to say anything about this, Mr. Dade. Me and the sheriff's going to head for the Boyd place right away."

"To arrest them, I hope," Dade said. "I don't like to think of thieves being left free in Bowie."

"My guess is we'll arrest 'em," Longarm said. "We'll be looking for some other evidence, but them slickers will go a long way to tie them to the train holdup."

Becker added, "Your evidence will go a long way to proving they're guilty. It'd be too bad if some smart lawyer from Fort Worth or Wichita Falls got them off because we didn't have it."

"That's why the sheriff wouldn't want you to talk about the slickers before the trial," Longarm said.

"Oh, I'll keep my mouth shut, don't worry about that," Dade promised. "I knew the Boyds were having trouble paying their bills, but I never would've thought they'd turn into outlaws."

Longarm turned to Becker. "We'd better be riding. I'd just as soon get there while there's plenty of daylight left, in case we run into trouble."

As they rode out of town, Longarm said to Becker, "Maybe you better tell me what you know about these Boyds."

"There's not much to tell," the sheriff replied. "Outside of getting drunk enough to make trouble once in a while, all I know about them is that they showed up about a year ago and made a dicker for that little spread they run."

"Any idea where they come from?"

"Some place back East. Missouri, as I recall."

"They ever talk about what they worked at before they showed up here?"

Becker shook his head. "They never talk about much of anything to anybody. They keep pretty much to themselves."

"You ever had to arrest 'em? You remarked that they made trouble sometimes when they was drunk."

"Oh, I had to put one of them—Joe, I think it was—in the lockup overnight once, to sober up when he got into a little fistfight with a drifting cowhand. I let both of them go the next morning without taking them to court, though."

An hour's ride brought Longarm and Becker within sight of a small shabby house and barn badly in need of repairs. The buildings stood a quarter of a mile off the trail, and there was no sign of activity around them. They turned their mounts onto the path that led to the house, and when they'd gotten to within a few hundred feet of them they could see what had been hidden from them at a distance. A man was at work building a haystack from a head-high wall of bales stacked beside the bars of a corral at the corner of the barn.

"That's one of the Boyds," Becker told Longarm. "I can't say yet whether it's Joe or Jeff. They look an awful lot alike."

Longarm slid his rifle out of its saddle scabbard. "Let's you and me spread out a little ways, Sheriff. Not borrowing trouble, but we won't make as good a target if we got a little daylight between us. Why don't you just ride on straight ahead, and I'll cut away toward the house."

When the Boyd brother pitching hay finally noticed Longarm and Becker riding up, he stopped and stared from one of them to the other. A few minutes later Longarm could tell that he must have recognized the sheriff, for he dropped his pitchfork and ran into the barn. A moment later a rifle cracked and its slug kicked up dirt a few yards behind Becker.

Spinning his horse, the sheriff widened the angle between himself and Longarm by spurring away at an angle, heading for the corner of the structure opposite the one which Longarm was approaching. Longarm had kicked his mount up when the shot rang out and was slanting his mount toward the corner of the house.

He had almost reached the corner of the house where the dwelling would have been between him and the barn when a second shot cracked and the slug from the rifle grazed his horse. With a shrill whinny of pain, the horse instinctively leaped forward. Longarm was behind the house before the

96

Boyd brother in the barn could trigger his weapon again.

As Longarm urged his limping mount around the house he heard the distinctive boom of a heavy-caliber rifle, followed by a splintering of wood, and knew that it had come from Becker's gun. There was silence then, a stillness that lasted long enough to give Longarm time to complete his circuit of the house and get to a point where he could see the barn once more. At the angle from which he was forced to look, Longarm could see the opening of the barn door only at an oblique angle, and he could not see inside the structure.

Past the barn, however, he had a clear view of the sheriff, who had dismounted and taken cover behind his horse. Longarm swung out of the saddle and inspected the hind foot which his horse was holding off the ground. He saw at first glance that the animal's wound was nothing more than a graze about its hoof. The horse would be able to move as soon as it had gotten over the shock of the bullet. He returned his attention to the Boyd brother in the barn.

There was no sign of movement in the narrow black slit of the barn's open door. Beyond the barn Becker was moving, holding his rifle ready. As Longarm watched him, he stepped from his cover and fired. The heavy slug crashed into the side of the barn. Longarm saw splinters fly as the lead drove through to the interior. A yowl of pain came from the open door. Longarm sprinted toward the sound.

He slid to a halt on the packed dirt of the barn floor as he saw the wounded man sprawled beside the wall. He was clutching one arm to his body, blood trickling down his wrist to the floor. His rifle lay a short distance away, its stock splintered. When the wounded man saw Longarm enter he made a move toward the rifle, but stopped and remained motionless when Longarm lifted the muzzle of his own weapon cover him.

"Stay right like you are!" Longarm snapped.

"All right! Just don't shoot me!" the man replied.

He watched as Longarm sidled to the rifle, swivelling to keep the threatening muzzle of his own weapon trained on him. As Longarm kicked the shattered stock of the fallen

97

gun out of reach, Becker came hurrying through the door.

"That was a nice shot, Sheriff," Longarm told him. "And since this fellow started shooting at us as soon as we got close enough for him to recognize you, that's a pretty good sign him and his brother's the men we're after."

"I don't know what you're talking about!" Boyd protested. "Me and Joe ain't done a thing!"

"Why'd you start shooting at me and the sheriff, then?" Longarm demanded. "Men that ain't afraid to see a law officer coming towards 'em don't act like that!"

"You've seen me around town enough times to know me, Jeff," Becker said. "Now suppose you tell us where we can find Joe?"

"All you got to do is turn around, Sheriff!" a new voice spoke from the door. "But I'll cut you down if you move a muscle till you've throwed down your guns and hoisted your hands!"

Becker let his rifle fall at once and started raising his hands. He was standing directly in front of Joe Boyd, while Longarm stood farther back. He cold see Boyd only in profile, and all but an edge of the outlaw's body was hidden by the door. Longarm realized immediately that if Boyd carried out his threat to shoot, the sheriff would be his first target.

"It's about time you got here, Joe!" Jeff Boyd said when he saw the sheriff's hands go up. As he spoke he started getting to his feet.

"Damn it, Jeff," Joe cried, swivelling to get Longarm in his sights, "stay down outa my way!"

His warning came too late. As soon as Longarm saw Becker toss his rifle down he had started raising his own weapon, gambling that in their preoccupation with the sheriff the brothers would not notice his own movement.

Echoes of Jeff Boyd's shot still reverberated in the barn when Longarm's finger closed on the trigger of his own weapon. A split-second later, Boyd's body jerked as the slug went home. His finger closed involuntarily on the trigger of his rifle, but the bullet whistled harmlessly past Becker and through the side wall of the barn. The recoil of his shot tore the weapon from Boyd's relaxing hands as his knees folded and he sagged to the floor beside his brother.

Joe Boyd reached for the fallen gun as it landed on the floor beside him. Longarm had anticipated the wounded man's move. He swivelled his Winchester and snapshot at Boyd's hand as it stretched for his brother's weapon.

Longarm's hasty, unaimed slug was off by a hair's-breadth. It did not strike the back of Boyd's moving hand, but grazed the web between his thumb and forefinger before burying itself in the ground. The graze was enough to cause Boyd to pull his hand back. By that time Longarm had pushed the muzzle of his Winchester into Boyd's cheek. The outlaw froze and stayed immobile.

"I give up!" he shouted. "Sheriff, tell this trigger-happy deputy of yours to get his damned rifle outa my face!"

"I can't give him orders," Becker said. "He's not my deputy. He's a U. S. marshal here to investigate that job of train robbing you and your brother pulled the other day."

"We didn't do no such thing!" Boyd protested, but the trembling of his voice gave the lie to his weak denial. "All right, Sheriff! I'll confess me and Jeff robbed that train if you just don't let this damn federal man kill me!"

Longarm kicked the rifle out of reach before moving his Winchester back just far enough to ease the pressure of its cold steel muzzle on Boyd's cheek. When Longarm spoke, his voice was as cold as the steel of the Winchester's muzzle.

"You got two ways to go," he told Boyd. "You can tell me where you hid what you stole off that train, or you can stall till I lose my patience and send you to join your brother."

Boyd made his choice quickly. "It's buried in that corner over there," he said, nodding to indicate the location. "It ain't very deep; you'll come to it about three inches under."

Longarm jerked his head at Becker. The sheriff walked over to the spot Boyd had indicated. A shovel leaned against the wall nearby and he picked it up and started digging. He'd turned only three or four shovelsful of dirt when the corner of a canvas mailbag showed.

"He wasn't lying this time," Becker said. "I guess this is all we need to close the case, Marshal Long."

As they rode back toward Bowie, Jeff Boyd's body lashed behind the saddle of the horse his brother was riding, Becker pulled up close to Longarm and asked him in a low voice, "Tell me something, Marshal. Would you really have shot Joe if he hadn't told us where that mailbag was?"

Longarm replied, "I never have cut down a man who didn't have a gun pointing my way, and I sure wouldn't've started with him."

By the time they had delivered Jeff Boyd's body to the undertaking parlor, had Joe Boyd's wounds attended to, and placed him in one of the cells in the rear of the sheriff's office, the day was fading into dusk. Longarm and Becker sat at a table in the Lady May. A bottle of Tom Moore stood in front of Longarm and one of Kentucky Dew bourbon in front of the sheriff.

"I've been in my job for over a year now," Becker said. "But in one day you've taught me more about what a lawman needs to know than I've learned since I was sworn in. I'd sure like to see you stay around awhile, Longarm."

"Oh, you'll learn all you need to know as times goes on," Longarm assured him. "I guess I picked up something new just about every case I take on. I learned something on this case myself."

"You mind telling me what?" the sheriff asked.

"Oh, it ain't no secret," Longarm replied. "I guess you know that I was pulled off of trying to catch up with this crook that's called the Kiowa Kid because you folks here thought he was the train robber."

"Well, it was a natural enough mistake," Becker protested. "Since he pulled that job in Chilicothe, everybody in these parts has been wondering where he'd pop up next."

"Sure, I grant you that," Longarm nodded. "But I've lost a lot of time when I oughta been trying to pick up his trail. It's got cold by now."

"Since he didn't pull off this job, how do you know where to look next?" the sheriff asked.

"Why, I don't. But I got a hunch that when he give me the slip up in Chilicothe, he cut a shuck for Indian Territory."

"Then you'll be leaving right away?"

Longarm nodded. "I'll be catching the northbound train

a little after midnight, and a long day's ride will get me to Fort Sill." He glanced over to the bar where May Morgan was standing. She raised her eyebrows questioningly and Longarm replied with an almost imperceptible nod. Turning back to Becker, he went on, "I got a mite of unfinished personal business to take care of tonight. But I got to ask a favor of you, Sheriff."

"Ask away, but you've got it before I even know what it is. It'd be pretty sorry of me to turn you down, after the way you helped me here."

"Well, there's a government rule that when us marshals need a horse, we're supposed to go to the closest army fort and requisition one. Fort Sill's the closest fort to Bowie, but there ain't no way to get to it on the train. I'd be much obliged for the loan of the horse and saddle gear I been using today. I fix it up with the remount officer at Fort Sill to get it back to you as quick as he can."

"You've got the horse," Becker nodded. "And anything else you need."

"That's all I can think of. And I do thank you."

Becker stood up. Longarm followed suit and the two men shook hands. "I'd better be getting along," the sheriff said. "I've got some unfinished business myself at the office."

Chapter 12

"I can't help it, Marshal Long," the remount sergeant said. "I'll fix you up with a horse and gear, but I can't put that nag of yours in a corral with our own stock. It's against regulations."

"Then just keep this nag of mine separate till you can figure a way to get it back down to Texas," Longarm suggested.

"There's not any way I can do that, either," the soldier replied. "We can't mix service horses with civilian ones; it's against regulations."

Longarm's temper was growing shorter by the minute. "Now, look here—" he began, then stopped short when he heard a hoarse growling voice call his name.

"Longarm! What in hell're you doing way down here in the Indian Nation? I heard you was working up in the Rockies!"

There was no need for Longarm to turn around. "Cass Masters! Why, I thought you'd settled down up in the Tetons by now, like you always said you was going to do!"

"Well, I did settle up there, Longarm," the grizzled new-comer replied. "Stuck it out through two winters. Then I hightailed it back to where winter jest lasts four or five months instead of six or eight."

Surveying Masters's chest-long beard and shoulder-length gray hair, Longarm said, "I see you didn't start going to the barber when you come back where it's warm."

"Hell, I'm too old to change my ways," the oldster grinned. "And, from what I just heard, you ain't changed, either. Still bound to get your way, come hell or high water. Now, let me give you a hand with this sojer boy." Turning to the remount sergeant, he said, "Sonny, just put Marshal Long's nag in the corral with my critters. That'll fit in with your damn fool regulations and maybe keep you outa trouble."

Turning to Longarm, the soldier asked, "Is that all right with you, Marshal?"

"Do what Cass tells you," Longarm said. "And fix a requisition for the horse I need. I'll come get it later." He turned back to Masters and went on, "Let's you and me go over to the sutler's and get a drink. I just stopped here to pick up a fresh horse."

"I was thinking about a drink myself," Cass said. "Are you just taking a pleasure trip, or chasing after somebody special?"

"I'm looking for whoever it is that's calling himself the Kiowa Kid these days," Longarm replied.

"Now hold on! The Kiowa Kid's dead." Masters frowned. "If I ain't wrong, you put him away yourself, up in Dakota Territory some time back."

Longarm nodded. "That's what I figured, too, but it seems like there's at least two more on the prod now."

"Here in the Nation?"

"That's what I aim to find out. Right now I'm heading for Lawton, to see Quanah Parker. He might be only half Comanche, but if there's anybody knows what's going on anyplace where there's Comanches or Kiowas, it'll be him."

"Well, you sure won't find him in Lawton, Longarm," Cass said. "I was gonna visit old Quanah when I first got back in these parts a few months ago, so I swung by that place he built for him and all them wives he'd picked up after he settled down, but the folks at the agency there told me he'd moved down to Greer County."

"Wait a minute, now!" Longarm said. "Don't tell me that Quanah's got himself mixed up in that boundary wrangle between Texas and the Indian Bureau."

"You mean you ain't heard he'd sidled into the fuss?"

"Land boundaries ain't quite in my line of work," Longarm replied. "The only reason I heard about it was when Billy Vail told me I might have to go down there if trouble started. Then, when he didn't say no more about it, I just took it for granted the fuss was settled without shooting."

"Well, there ain't been shooting trouble down there, but it ain't been settled, either. The Comanches leased that part of their reservation to a bunch of ranchers who was running short of good grazing range. If Texas gets all that Greer County land, they'll either have to buy it or pay the state grazing fees for using it."

"They got a better deal from the Comanches than they could from their own people?" Longarm asked.

"Oh, not by much, maybe a dollar a year a head better, but you figure how much more they'd be out for twenty or thirty thousand head a year."

"And the Comanches will be outa pocket by a pretty sizeable amount," Longarm said. "You don't need to go no further. I can figure out what happened. Quanah having white blood makes him the one them cattlemen would be likely to get along best with, so the other chiefs got him to move down there."

"Something like that," Cass said. "Anyways, if you want to talk to Quanah Parker, you'll have a leetle more travelling to do. What do you need to talk to old Quanah about, anyhow?"

"This case I'm on. I'm after an outlaw that calls himself the Kiowa Kid, and since the Kiowas has always been sorta partners with the Comanches, I figure if anybody'd know where he's got himself holed up, it'd be Quanah."

"Well, you're right about that," Cass agreed. "After

Mackenzie whupped the Comanches in Palo Duro Canyon, Quanah's the one that kept the young bloods together till after that fight at Adobe Walls. Even after he was beat there, the young Comanche men mostly cottoned to him, so he's got spies all over the whole damn Indian Nation."

"That being the way of it, I'm going to have some more riding to do," Longarm said. He glanced at the sun dropping toward the horizon. "And I've had more'n my share just getting up here from Texas. Looks like I better stay here at the fort tonight, and get a fresh start in the morning. So we'll have a chance to swap a few stories. If I get an early start tomorrow and push hard, I oughta get where I'm heading right after dark."

Longarm rode out of Fort Sill the following morning and put the red sunrise at his back. His sinewy body was refreshed by the first full night of sleep he had had in several days. When his evening of talking with Cass, catching up on old times, and tossing down a few drinks had ended, he had slept like a baby in a tolerable bed in the bachelor officers' quarters. The breakfast of ham and eggs and garrison bread at the officers' mess had brought his stomach to a satisfied glow. The chestnut gelding the remount sergeant had delivered to him was fresh, and he was comfortable being back in a familiar McClellan saddle again.

Longarm found it pleasant to give the gelding its head and let it move at its own easy pace. The only problem he could see ahead was to find a safe place to cross the Red River when the time came for him to angle over toward Quanah Parker's settlement.

This country's changing fast, old son, he mused as he rode along. *It don't look the same as it did last time you paid a call on old Quanah. But I guess things can't ever stay the same.*

He toed the horse to a faster pace as the sun rose higher. When the sun stood overhead, he pulled up at a little run, a tiny whisper of water almost hidden by the prairie grass. Dismounting, Longarm took off the chestnut's halter to let the animal graze and drink while he ate.

Back in the saddle, Longarm rode with increasing urgency as the afternoon waned. He reached the Canadian River in mid-afternoon. Having had experience with the stream's notoriously treacherous bottom, he followed its winding bank on the north side until the houses of the tiny village where the wily old Comanche chief had resettled came into sight on the opposite bank.

Even with the village in sight, Longarm did not try to ford the river until he saw hoofprints and the ruts of wagon wheels leading down the gentle slope to the water's edge, marking a safe spot to cross. Longarm walked the chestnut into the tiny little town. Actually, it was too small to be called a town; there were fewer than a dozen houses extending along one side of the trail. Near the center of the row, only distinguishable from the houses on either side by its hitch rail and the half-story false front with a tin-covered awning spanning its facade, there was a store.

One thing's certain-sure, old son, Longarm told himself, *you won't have no trouble finding Quanah in a place as little as this one, even if he still puts them six wives of his in six different houses.*

As he neared the store, he saw that finding the Comanche leader would be easier than he had thought. Quanah Parker was sitting on a bench under the store's awning.

Longarm reined in and dismounted and tossed the chestnut's reins over the hitch rail. As he walked up to the store his eyes flicked quickly over the Comanche leader. Quanah was watching Longarm at the same time, but his face did not reveal either surprise, a hint of welcome, or displeasure.

Quanah Parker's appearance gave little hint that he was of mixed Indian and white blood. He had the broad face, wide jaw, and high cheekbones of the Comanche people. The only vestige of his mother's blood showed in his lips, which were thinner than those of most full-blood Comanches, his higher brow-line and aquiline nose. He wore the serge trousers and vest of a business suit and a collarless white shirt.

"Howdy," Longarm said as he walked up to the edge of the porch. Quanah Parker nodded, but said nothing. Longarm went on, "I don't know if you recall meeting me before, because it's been awhile back, but—"

"You are the federal marshal named Long," Quanah said quietly. "You have another name, too; it is Longarm."

"That's right," Longarm nodded.

Quanah went on, "You came to me to ask about the Comancheros that were causing trouble far to the south, on the *llano estacado*."

"That was a good while back," Longarm said. He sat down on the edge of the porch, leaned against one of its supporting pillars, and dug two cheroots from his vest pocket. He offered one to Quanah, who shook his head.

Quanah waited until Longarm settled back after lighting his cigar, then he said, "You did a good thing for my people by proving Comanches were not to blame. We think of you as a friend, Longarm. You are welcome in our *tipis*." Quanah stopped and shook his head and a smile flicked his lips. "Or our houses. Sit down, and we will talk of whatever brings you to me now."

"I'll say this, Chief Quanah, you sure got a good memory," Longarm remarked.

"My people must remember things," the Comanche replied. "It is only now that our young men are learning to write. But you did not come to talk about such things. Have some of our people committed crimes against the federal laws?"

"None that I know about," Longarm replied, "unless you count the Kiowas as being the same tribe as Comanches."

Quanah was silent for a moment, his face immobile. Longarm waited patiently, knowing the Indians' way of remaining silent at any time they chose to, even during a friendly conversation.

"Some of our men have married Kiowa women," he said at last. "And some Kiowa men have married Comanche women. Many of their children call themselves Comanche–Kiowas or Kiowa–Comanches. But I am sure you know this."

"I've heard about it," Longarm nodded. "And I ain't right sure if the man I'm after is a full-blood or not. He might be part white, for all I know. But you'd know him by the name he travels under; he calls himself the Kiowa Kid."

Quanah nodded. "Yes. It is not a strange name. There has been more than one who has called himself that. But you know of them. Some years ago you killed one in the Dakota country."

"This is a new one," Longarm said. "And I'm right sure he was headed into the Nation when he killed a town marshal down in Chilicothe. He's the one I'm here to bring in."

"You won't find him in the Nation, Longarm," Quanah said. "I know of the man. I think he has no Kiowa blood. He was on the Kiowa land to the east of here a week or more ago. The Kiowa do not recognize him as belonging to their tribe. They told him to leave."

"Which I guess he did?"

"I have not heard. But he would have been a fool to stay."

"Whether he was really Kiowa or not?"

"Of course. If the elders banished him, no Kiowa would give him shelter or try to hide him. Not even if he was a full-blood. And life is too hard on the small range we Comanches and Kiowas have now. When the beef your government gives us does not arrive on time, we go hungry."

"I've heard about that," Longarm said.

Quanah said, "It was not long ago that you helped our old enemies the Cheyennes to get beef from a crooked agent."

Accustomed as he was to keeping a poker face, Longarm kept his surprise from showing. "You mean you heard about that run-in I had with a crooked Indian agent up in Colorado?" he asked.

"Of course." For the first time, Quanah let an emotion show when he smiled at Longarm's question. His smile flickered across his broad face for only a fraction of a second. Then he went on, his voice very serious, "We talk with our old enemies now, Longarm. If we had started talking to each other before my force attacked Adobe Walls, there would have not been a fight in Palo Duro, and your people would not be on our land now."

Before Longarm could come up with a question or remark that would have bridged the awkward silence that followed, Quanah was speaking again. "You're in the Nation to find the Kiowa Kid, you said. I can't give you much help in that."

Longarm said, "A minute ago you told me I wasn't likely to find the Kiowa Kid anyplace in the Nation. You feel like telling me anything else?" When Quanah did not answer at once, Longarm added, "I can sure use some help, Quanah. It ain't doing your friends the Kiowas no good for a killer like him to use the name of their tribe."

"Yes, that is true," Quanah said.

He was silent again for a few seconds, and this time Longarm realized that any more urging on his part would be useless.

"Look for him in the Panhandle, Longarm," Quanah went on when he finally broke his silence.

"You got any advice where I oughta start?"

"Texas is your people's land. You know that all Comanches must have permission from our agent to leave the Nation, and I do not choose to ask." When Longarm did not comment, Quanah added, "I hear things, of course, but you know just as I do where the outlaws like to go."

"Tascosa?" Longarm asked. When Quanah did not answer or change expression he tried again. "Mobeetie?"

"Outlaws of your people and ours can be found in both of them." Quanah nodded, his voice still expressionless.

Longarm realized that Quanah Parker would give him no more information. "Sure. And there's other towns in the Panhandle where outlaws goes, too. I reckon I got sense enough to find the Kiowa Kid, or run across a trail I can pick up."

When Quanah nodded but did not speak, Longarm decided it was time for him to go. "This time I owe you, Quanah," he said. "I know you ain't likely to need no help, but if you ever do—"

Quanah nodded again, cutting short Longarm's offer. His broad face remained expressionless.

"Well, I guess I better get moving again before it gets too dark to see," Longarm said, glancing at the sky.

"If you return, you will be welcome as a friend," Quanah said. "But do not wear your badge when you come in friendship."

"I'll remember," Longarm replied. He stood up, stretched, and said, "Till next time."

He did not wait for Quanah to reply, but walked to the hitch rail, picked up the reins of the chestnut, and swung into the saddle. He rode off and did not look back.

Chapter 13

His horse fresh from its rest during his long conversation with Quanah Parker, Longarm set a faster pace than he had maintained earlier in the day. He was back now in country that he knew from earlier cases, and could plan his movements without wasting time worrying about directions and distances. Since he knew that Tascosa was a four-day ride and he could reach Mobeetie in two days of hard riding, he began angling north soon after leaving Quanah's village.

Longarm made good time. He made an overnight camp on the banks of a little creek tht flowed into the Salt Fork of the Red River and splashed across the shallow, sluggish Salt Fork itself late the next day. That night he spread his bedroll beside Elm Fork, with Mobeetie now only a short day ahead.

By high noon the following day Longarm was pushing through the hummocky brakes of the Red River's North Fork. After he had urged the chestnut gelding up the zigzag trail that mounted the high bluff marking the north edge of the creased and broken bottomland he stopped to breathe

the horse. In front of him the prairie flattened out as flat as the top of a broad table, showing nothing but an expanse of short bunchgrass rippling in the gentle breeze to the straight unbroken rim of the horizon.

Progress was fast across the flat tableland, and Longarm could almost lounge in his saddle while the chestnut ate up the distance in an easy canter. An hour after he had crossed the Red's North Fork, the monotony of the featureless prairie was broken when he reached the military road that connected Fort Supply with Fort Elliott.

Stretching string-straight across the gently upsloping prairie, the long grassless strip looked inviting. Longarm reined the chestnut onto it, but the criss-crossing ruts cut into its surface by the tall wheels of the big army supply wagons were so deep that the gelding began breaking stride when its feet slid into them. Longarm soon pulled the reins to turn the animal back onto the smoother surface of the prairie.

When the tops of Mobeetie's houses broke the line of level ground ahead, the sun still hung a full handspan above their tops. Gauging the distance between the level horizon and the slowly yellowing sun, Longarm judged that when he covered the remaining distance to Mobeetie there would still be more than an hour of daylight left.

Plenty of time to take a look at the town before dark, and still get out to Fort Elliott in time for supper. Army grub might not be much more'n gut-wadding, but it sure beats that greasy stuff them Mexican cooks in that cafe in Mobeetie was dishing up last time you was here.

When the narrow, rutted wagon road widened into a street of packed yellow soil with houses on each side, Longarm reined his mount to a slow walk. What had been concealed by distance could be seen readily at close hand, and before he had ridden fifty yards along the street Longarm began frowning. One out of every three of the houses he passed was unoccupied, the windows shuttered or boarded up. On his earlier visits he had not seen even one vacant house.

When he reached the main street and turned to ride down it he could see even more plainly that what had been a

112

booming town was settling into the first stages of desertion that would lead to its death. There were only three or four buckboards moving along a street which had once been crowded. Fresh boards were nailed across the swinging doors of a saloon, and though the next three saloons were open, only a horse or two stood at their hitch rails.

Gaping, sashless windows stared from two half-finished brick buildings on opposite corners. Beyond them Longarm saw the batwings of a saloon. He turned the chestnut to the empty hitch rail and flipped the reins around it, then went inside. The bar was empty except for the bartender, who was dozing in a chair. When he heard Longarm's boot heels thudding on the floor he let the front legs of his chair drop to the floor and stood up.

"What'll it be, friend?" he asked, wiping the mahogany with his apron.

"Maryland rye whiskey, if you got any," Longarm said. "Tom Moore is what I favor."

"It happens we've got plenty of Moore," the barkeep replied. "Plenty of everything else, too, except customers." He wiped dust off the bottle with his apron and put it on the mahogany in front of Longarm. Turning to the neatly stacked glasses he reached for a small shotglass, then moved his hand down to the section where water tumblers stood and took one off a stack. As he put the glass in front of Longarm, he went on, "Double shots for the price of one, friend. Help yourself."

Longarm tossed a coin on the bar. "Business that bad, is it?"

"Slow as molasses in wintertime," the barkeep nodded. "But it's sure to pick up soon as roundup's over and the trail herds start to move."

"From what I seen when I was riding in, I'd say your town's been on a downhill drag for quite a while," Longarm commented.

"Oh, things have slowed down, all right."

"What d'you figure's happened?" Longarm asked.

"Well, nobody seems to be able to figure it out," the barkeep replied. "Everything just begun to slow down after

113

some English outfit bought the Maple Leaf, and then they bought out the T Bar T a little while later. And there's another English outfit bought up the Long S, down in the south part of the county, and when they both begun hiring new hands, our regulars just drifted away."

"That could have something to do with it," Longarm nodded. He took another swallow of the rye. "I guess when things begun to fall off you lost a lot of drifters and some of the shady characters and suchlike riffraff that used to come into town?"

"Some of 'em, sure. But there's always plenty of that kind to go around."

Longarm nodded and picked up his change. "I'll stop in next time I'm in town. Tom Moore's hard to find sometimes, and I don't cotton to that sweet Pennsylvania rye or bourbon."

"If you feel like buying a bottle to take along with you, I've got six cases in my storeroom, and I'll sell you a bottle for a lot less than it'd cost you paying by the drink."

"Maybe next time. But thanks for the offer, anyhow."

When Longarm left the saloon, the long twilight of the high plains was near. He rode north out of town, splashed across Sweet Water Creek, and before the chestnut gelding had worked the stiffness out of its legs the sprawled-out adobe buildings of Fort Elliott were in sight. There was no sentry in the weatherbeaten, coffin-like box that stood at the point where the road curved into the cluster of buildings, and no sign of life anywhere along the wide avenues that separated the abode structures.

Longarm looked around until he saw the regimental guidon that marked the headquarters building. He walked the chestnut over to it, swung out of the saddle, and went inside. A soldier sat at a table just inside the door, but the desks in the room were all unoccupied. The soldier looked up when Longarm entered and sat a bit more erectly in his chair when he saw the visitor.

Stopping at the table, Longarm said, "I'm a deputy United States marshal, my name's Long, and I need to have a word with your commanding officer."

"That'd be Major Hastings, sir. He's in the officers' mess having supper right now."

"I'll walk over and find him myself," Longarm replied. "I been here before; I know my way around."

"Yes, sir," the soldier nodded. "I guess that's all right."

Angling across the drillground, Longarm entered the mess hall. Two rows of small square tables stood spaced with military precision down the center of the long, narrow room. There were a dozen or so officers in field uniform sitting at them, but it took only a moment for Longarm to pick out the gold oakleaves of the major from the silver bars of the lower ranks. He made his way to the table, eyes following him. Stopping beside the major's chair, Longarm repeated the stock introduction he had used so many times before.

"I imagine you've dropped in to take potluck with us, Marshal Long," the major said. "Glad to have you. We see damned few strange faces here at mealtime unless there's a supply train in."

"I ain't just passing through, Major," Longarm replied. "I expect I'll be here a day or so. I got to do some looking around in Mobeetie, and it might take me a while."

"We'll have a chance to talk, then," Hastings said. "Find yourself a chair and sit down while there's still some hot food in the kitchen. We'll talk after supper."

"Thanks, but I better see to my horse first," Longarm told the major. "I've spent a little time here before now, so I'll just take him out to the stables before I set down to eat."

"Feel free to join us at the officers' club later, Hastings said. "If you've been here before you'll know it's not much, but it's the only one we've got."

"As I recall, you didn't have an officers' club last time I was here," Longarm replied. "But I only passed through that time. I did get to eat at your mess hall, and slept in some officer's bed that he wasn't using because he was off on some kinda job."

"Well, the club's just two buildings from this one, toward the sally port. Drop in when you've finished your meal."

"I'll do that," Longarm replied. "And if your provost

marshal should happen to be there, too, I'd be glad of a chance to talk to him a few minutes."

"I'll see that he's there," Hastings nodded. "And Lieutenant Blake over there is officer of the day; he'll see to it that you've got a place to sleep. We've got a couple of rooms for transient officers now, and I suppose you'd fall into that category."

"Thanks, Major," Longarm said. "Now I won't keep you from your supper any longer."

Fort Elliott's officers' club was a contrast of the new and the old. The furniture was an unlikely mixture of kitchen chairs and a few fine upholstered chairs that had obviously come from the East; the two tables were the same as those in the mess, and a large cabinet had the look of having been made by a ranch artisan.

Longarm was sitting at a table in one corner of the room with Major Hastings and Lieutenant Smothers, the fort's provost marshal. Hastings saw Longarm examining the place by the yellow light that came from two lanterns hanging from its ceiling and said, "If our clubroom looks like it's been put together from scraps, that's because it was, Marshal Long. I guess you know that army doesn't provide for facilities of this kind."

"As a matter of fact, I didn't," Longarm replied. "But it looks like it'll be right nice when you finish it."

"It's better than sitting in our quarters or the mess hall," Smothers put in. "And those of us who do our work in the headquarters office don't get much change of scenery. But you said you're on a case here, Marshal Long. Do you expect to be here for awhile?"

"I figured I might be when I started out for here," Longarm replied. "But what I seen when I rode through Mobeetie on my way here has sorta changed my mind. What's happened to that town, anyhow? Looks to me like it's sort dying on the vine."

"It is right now," Hastings agreed. "I don't guess you've had time to look around the fort, since you got here so late."

116

"I wasn't paying no special attention to it," Longarm replied. "But I was here a couple of years back, and I didn't notice it's changed much."

"Oh, we've still got all the buildings that were put up while the army was busy with the redskins," Hastings said. "But the fact is that since General Mackenzie whipped the Comanches down at Palo Duro Canyon, the brass in Washington's been whittling away at the forts in Texas and the Indian Nation."

"I guess the War Department figures they can cut down some, now the Comanches ain't kicking up a fuss?" Longarm asked.

"Yes, they've made that clear," Hastings nodded. "Now they're sending more and more men to Arizona Territory and New Mexico Territory, and to southwest Texas. The Apaches are getting most of the attention now that the Comanches and Kiowas are whipped."

"Well, I reckon that makes sense," Longarm said. "But it ain't Indians that's brought me down here, Major. There's a pesky outlaw that calls himself the Kiowa Kid, and he's the one I'm after. I got a hint he might've cut a shuck for Mobeetie, so I figured I might pick up his tracks here."

"Well, Mobeetie had more than its share of outlaws and badmen until a little while ago," Smother said. "They even set up a sort of Robbers' Roost on Red Deer Creek, eight or ten miles to the northwest. From what I've heard, Billy the Kid used it now and then."

"What's it like now?" Longarm asked. "Do the outlaws still hole up in it?"

Smothers shook his head. "It's supposed to be abandoned now, but I haven't been up there for a year or so."

"Did your men clean it up?" Longarm asked.

Hastings said, "The army never was asked to. The cattle association regulators took care of the job. I don't know too much about it, because that was before I got posted here."

"Now, that sounds like the kind of place the man I'm after would cotton to," Longarm frowned. "He'd be wanting a place to lay low, because I found out when I stopped in the Indian Nation on my way up here that the Kiowas and the Comanches wouldn't take him in."

"If you want to ride up there in the morning, I'll be glad to go with you," Smothers volunteered. "With the major's permission, of course."

"You might as well be helping the marshal as sitting at your desk with nothing to do," Hastings said. "If Marshal Long wants you to guide him, I don't have any objections."

"It'll save me wasting a lot of time trying to find the place," Longarm told Smothers. "I don't figure it'd do me much good to go into Mobeetie till evening. I'll take you up on your offer, Lieutenant."

"We'll be there in another few minutes, now," Lieutenant Smothers told Longarm as they rode in single file up the bed of a dry creek.

"I can sure see why a bunch of outlaws would cotton to a place like this," Longarm said. He looked at the sheer rock walls cut by the water of the long-dead stream. The canyon's sides towered high above their heads. "A couple of men with rifles could stand off an army in this canyon."

"It opens into a box canyon ahead," Smothers volunteered. "The canyon's not big, but it'll hold a dozen or more men and horses."

"I ain't seen any sign that somebody's been here for quite a while, though." Longarm frowned. "No hoofprints, no horse droppings."

"We may be on a fool's chase," the lieutenant said. "But I can't think of a better place for a wanted man to hide."

They rounded a sharp bend in the narrow passageway and found themselves in a box canyon. Its walls were steep and a layer of sand covered the floor.

At first Longarm could see no evidence that the place had ever been used, but as they rode across the canyon he spotted several places where rocks had been arranged in circles to accommodate cooking fires. When he looked at these closely he saw that not even any long-dead coals were left in them. The sandy canyon floor was bare of hoofprints.

"It looks like I led you out here on a waterhaul, Marshal," Smothers apologized as they headed out the cut.

"Well, it ain't exactly been time wasted," Longarm told his companion. "If we hadn't checked out this place and the Kiowa Kid was using it, we'd've missed him. But I'll say one thing about it: if I was on the run by myself, this is the last place I'd pick to hole up. All a posse'd have to do is wait for a man's grub and water to give out, and they'd have him."

"I hadn't thought about getting out," Smothers said, "but you're right. That may be why the outlaws gave it up after the men from the cattle association pulled their raid."

"I heard a little bit about that outfit Colonel Goodnight's been putting together," Longarm said. "And he ain't a man that'd hire anybody but the best hands he could find."

"They certainly cleaned up the country around Mobeetie," Smothers agreed. "And that's one reason the town's gone downhill of late. Of course, cutting down on our manpower at the fort has hurt business there, too."

"Then you don't keep a finger on things in town the way you used to?" Longarm asked.

Smothers shook his head. "There's not much to keep a finger on. Most of the trouble we had with our men was in the saloons and down in the red-light district. There aren't all that many places left where a soldier can get into a fracas."

"Mobeetie sure ain't the same town it was last time I was here," Longarm said. "But it just being a lot quieter now might be one of the things that'd draw the Kiowa Kid to it. Anyhow, I'm still aiming to nosey around some there later on today, most likely a little before sundown."

"If you don't run across the trail of the man you're after, you'll go on to Tascosa?"

"Oh, sure. Or anyplace else where I figure I got a chance at nabbing him."

"I haven't mentioned it before," Smothers said, "but from what I've heard Tascosa's really had a spurt ahead. There's talk of the Fort Worth & Denver building a new branch west

119

off their main line, and it's supposed to go through Tascosa."

"Well, that'd put it on the map, all right," Longarm nodded. "And if I don't smell out something this evening about the Kiowa Kid, Tascosa's the next place I'll go to look for him."

Chapter 14

Longarm waited until the shank of the afternoon, when the sun was almost touching the horizon, before going out for his look at Mobeetie.

Feeling at peace with the world, he walked the chestnut down the road from the fort to Mobeetie in the golden rays of the declining sun, splashed across Sweet Water Creek, and entered the town. He was lifting the reins to turn the chestnut onto the main business street when a thought struck him. Pulling the horse around in a half-circle, he started back toward the creek.

Just before reaching the stream he turned the chestnut onto a ragged path that looked as though it saw little use. He reached a house standing alone, closer to the creek than to the other dwellings. It was a house Longarm remembered well, and though he'd seen it only once by daylight he recognized it immediately. On two previous trips to Mobeetie he had spent memorably pleasant hours in it, with Sara Renfro on his first visit and her niece Sally on the second.

It was no longer the neat, trim house that he remembered. The pain was peeling, one of the columns that supported the small veranda had given way, two panes of glass were missing from the fanlight above the door, and the door and the window had been boarded up. Reining in, Longarm gazed at the house for a moment or two, then toed the chestnut into motion again and started toward Mobeetie's center.

He rode slowly, noticing how many of the stores had been boarded up or simply stood with their windows staring vacantly at the street, bare of merchandise displays, and how few people were moving around during what should have been the before-closing rush. When he had seen enough, he left the chestnut at the hitch rail in front of the Texas House and glanced around the vacant lobby as he crossed it to the bar.

Except for two men wearing Eastern-cut business suits and derbies who sat at a table near the free lunch counter, the place was deserted. Flipping a coin on the bar, he ordered his usual rye and left the change on the mahogany while he took his drink to the free lunch counter and filled a plate with cold meats, cheese, and a few pickles.

By the time he had finished making his selections his glass was almost empty. He returned to the bar, set down his plate, tossed off the whiskey remaining in his glass, and tapped it on the bar to signal for a refill.

"You folks set out a pretty good lunch," he remarked conversationally when the barkeep returned with his glass.

"Glad you like it, friend. You better enjoy it, because after this week there won't be no more," the barkeep said.

"I noticed things has slowed down since the last time I stopped off here," Longarm nodded. "How'd it come about?"

"That's what everybody wants to know," the man replied. "Me, I blame the limeys that's been buying up all the little ranches and making one big spread out of 'em. There's been a lot of that going on lately, and plenty of the hands has lost their jobs on account of it."

Longarm nodded. "I can see that. It don't take many more hands to run a big spread than it does a little one."

Nodding, the barkeep said, "Then the Rangers made a sweep in town and rousted out what they call the undesirables. Well, any fool knows that where the men goes, the girls down in the district just naturally follows. So when what hands are left on the spreads draw their pay they go to Tascosa now instead of coming in here to Mobeetie like they used to."

"That'd account for it, all right," Longarm agreed.

He ate the last piece of cheese, finished his drink, and walked out to the hitch rail. Dusk had taken the sky while he was in the salon, and darkness was near. Lights were shining in the section east of the business area where the saloons were thickest. They formed a sort of buffer zone between the business section and the cribs and parlor houses that stood beyond them at the edge of town.

Longarm walked the chestnut down the street. Few horses stood in front of the saloons. The tinkle of a player piano reached his ears and he reined up in front of the saloon from which the music came. After listening a moment, he toed his horse up to the hitch rail, secured the reins, and went inside.

In addition to the aproned barkeep there were two men standing near the center, their heads together in a low-voiced conversation. Longarm walked past them to the end of the mahogany. Behind the bar, the barkeep kept pace with him and stopped when Longarm stopped.

"Rye," Longarm said. He tossed a coin on the bar. "If it's Maryland rye I'll like it better, and if you got Tom Moore, that'll be better yet."

"I think I got some," the barkeep said.

He turned and began looking at the labels on the shelves behind the bar. A call-bell stood on one of the shelves and before moving toward the front of the building in search of the rye the man tapped it. Halfway down the bar, the barkeep took a bottle from the shelf and started back. Longarm was watching him when his ears caught the sound of a doorknob clicking. He swivelled quickly, his fingers curving, ready to draw.

A woman came through the door; she wore a low-cut

dress with a knee-length skirt that identified her as a saloon girl. Her back was to Longarm while she closed the door, and when she turned toward him Longarm's eyes opened wide and he let his hand fall to his side.

"Sara?" he asked. "Sara Renfro!"

"Longarm!" Sara gasped. "You're the last person I expected to see!" She stopped suddenly, then turned and started to go back through the door.

Longarm reached her side in one long stride and took her arm. "Hold on, Sara. If you don't want to talk to me, say so. But if you think maybe I don't want to talk to you, you're wrong."

Sara stared at him wide-eyed for a moment. Then Longarm felt the tense muscles of her arm relax.

"I—I guess I was just surprised," she told him. "I'd like to talk to you, of course. But not in here," She turned to the barkeep and said, "The other girls will be here in a few minutes, and it's so early you aren't likely to miss me for a little while." Without waiting for him to reply she turned back to Longarm and went on. "Come on. I don't live but a step or two from here."

Sara led Longarm down a long corridor to a side door that let them out into the darkness. "This way," she said, taking his arm. "I've got a room where we can talk without anybody interrupting us. It won't be like the house I used to have, but it's the best I can do right now. In case you're wondering, I don't belong to anybody now. After my arrangement with the officers at Fort Elliott fell apart, I swore—"

"You don't need to explain nothing to me, Sara," Longarm interrupted. "I'm just glad to see you again. I was wondering about you and Sally when I got to Mobeetie, but all the men out at the fort are new since I was here before, and there wasn't one of 'em I could ask. I rode by your house when I was coming into town tonight, sorta figured Sally might still be there, but she wasn't. It looked sorta dilapidated, and I gave up."

"It's been standing vacant since Sally left."

"Where's Sally now?"

"She's married and lives back East. I get a letter from her now and then."

"What about you?"

"When I left to go back to the reservation, I was positive I could be an Indian again, but it just didn't work. Maybe if I was even half-blood instead of quarter-blood I could've stood it, but..." She stopped, and took his hand again, and led him through a yard to a small house that stood silhouetted a few steps from the alley. Unlocking the door, she led him inside. "I'll light the lamp. Just stand here a minute."

The room he entered was small and sparsely furnished, too small to accommodate more than a narrow bureau and washstand, two straight chairs, and a double bed. Sara turned away from the lamp and saw him looking around.

"It's not much, but it's clean and I try to keep it neat," she said. "And the landlady minds her own business."

"It looks fine to me," Longarm told her.

he took off his hat and put it on the table. Turning back to Sara, he looked at her closely for the first time. Her honey-colored hair was a shade darker than when he'd seen her first, and there were a few faint lines etched at the corners of her full, pouting lips and at the corners of her eyes, but they were still as black and mysterious as ever under her dark eyebrows.

"You're just as pretty as ever, Sara," Longarm told her. "Maybe even prettier."

"You're not going to lecture me about what I'm doing?" she asked.

"Why in tunket do you think I'd do that? You're a full-grown woman. You know what you want to do."

"That's what I keep saying to myself," she said. Her voice still held the trace of defiance Longarm remembered. "I was a whore to just a few men before, but I suppose it's not any worse or better now, when I take on anybody who pays my price."

"You're still your own woman, and a real nice one, too, as far as I'm concerned."

Sara almost leaped into his arms. "Oh, I was hoping you'd say something like that, Longarm! I'll tell you, I've

125

never had a lover like you. Right now all I can think about is how much you've got to give a woman. Get your clothes off, quick!"

Longarm was slower in undressing than Sara was. She had shrugged out of her low-cut dress and pulled her long stockings off in a single quick move while he was getting out of his coat and vest and gunbelt. She saw Longarm's eyes on her as he took off his shirt and sat down to lever his boots off. She raised her hands and began to whirl around slowly.

When Longarm saw her full breasts bobbing he forgot his boots for a moment and sat staring at her. Sara stopped twirling and stepped up to him to help him get off his boots. Then she pulled his trousers and balbriggans off with one long jerk. Longarm had begun to swell. Sara took his hand. "Now, Longarm!" she said eagerly. "Take me to bed, quick!"

Longarm did not wait to carry Sara to the bed. He grasped her slim waist and lifted her off the floor, then held her suspended in front of him while she reached down between her outspread thighs to grasp his shaft and position him.

He began pulling her to him slowly, and Sara writhed as he slowly sank into her until their bodies met. Locking her legs around his waist, she began trying to pull him still deeper, and only then did Longarm take the two steps necessary to reach the bed. He lowered her until he felt his balance shifting when they were still above the bed. Then he fell forward on her and Sara cried out in a throaty sob as his full weight bearing down on her completed his penetration.

Longarm drove in quick, short strokes that brought throaty cries of pleasure from Sara's lips. Bit by bit he speeded his stroking, and when she started gasping with throaty, sobbing cries he drove harder and faster until she screamed into her climax. Her body tensed in a wild, rocking spasm before she gave a final loud, hoarse gasp and lay limp and quiet.

Longarm held himself pressed against her until he felt her stir and sigh. She clasped his head between her hands and pulled it down until she could reach his lips. Their tongues twined into a long kiss. While their lips were still glued together, Longarm began stroking again in a slow, deliberate rhythm of deep penetrations.

Soon Sara was rocking her hips in time to his deliberate thrusts. Longarm speeded up, and Sara matched his faster tempo until they were rocking together in the beginning of another orgasm. As Sara's cries reached their peak, Longarm let himself go. They shuddered and sighed as the waves of feeling swept through their bodies. Then their muscles relaxed, and the waves of feeling ebbed, and they both lay still.

Longarm felt Sara stirring and rolled off her to release her from his weight. He padded to his vest for a cigar and match, lighted up, and stretched out beside her again. As soon as he had settled down, Sara snuggled up to him and laid her head on the mat of course curls that covered his chest.

"That's the best thing that's happened to me since we were in bed together the last time," she signed contentedly.

"You're some kinda woman, Sara. I'm real glad I stopped in at that saloon when I did."

"So am I," she told him. "I was feeling pretty blue and lonesome. You're just the medicine I needed to cheer me up, and I hope you're going to stay in Mobeetie awhile."

"I sure hate to disappoint you, but I'm figuring to move on tomorrow. The fellow I'm looking for ain't likely to be here any longer, so I got to head for Tascosa."

"Who're you after now?" she asked. "Maybe I can help you."

"Well, the fellow I'm after is travelling under the name of the Kiowa Kid. I ain't got no idea what his real name is, but I'd guess he's likely to be part Kiowa."

Sara frowned as she said, "I don't remember anybody using that name being in Mobeetie. But, since you're going to Tascosa, maybe I can give you a little help after all. One of my best friends moved there a little while back."

"I can use all the help I can get," Longarm told her. "How do I go about finding her?"

"Her name's Frenchy. At least, that's the only name she'd ever give me. But the fellow she left to be with has a livery

127

stable there. His name's Mickey McCormick."

"I oughta be able to run her down without too much trouble, then," Longarm said thoughtfully. "Tascosa ain't all that big a town, as I recall it."

"It's grown a lot lately, they say," Sara told him. "But Frenchy's been there long enough to learn her way around."

"I'll find her. Don't worry," Longarm said. "And I owe you for your help, Sara. I ain't going to—"

"You don't owe me a thing, Longarm," Sara broke in. "But the night's not going to last forever, and for the last few minutes I haven't been able to put my mind on what we're saying." She slid her hand down to stroke his shaft. "All I can think of is that we're wasting time talking."

"I ain't one to waste time," Longarm replied. "If you're ready for us to start again, so am I."

"Lie still, then," she said, rising on her knees and bending down over him. "As soon as I get you up again, I'm going to straddle you and ride you until we're both too tired to do anything but sleep until the sun comes up."

Chapter 15

Longarm reined in a dozen yards from the point where the waters of the Canadian River met the prairie and gazed at the rippling greenish surface of the stream. The bank seemed solid enough, so he walked the chestnut down to the water's edge. Turning in the saddle to get the rays of the sun out of his eyes, he lighted a cheroot while the horse drank.

He scanned the country while waiting for the animal to finish drinking, but saw little that differed from the flat featureless terrain across which he had been riding since he turned to the northwest after leaving the army supply road that led from Fort Elliott to Fort Bascom.

Aside from a few places where a curve was necessary to avoid the deep slash of a canyon or an extensive rock outcrop, or to bring the road near a creek that would provide water for the wagon mules, its rutted surface ran string-straight. After he had turned off the military road in mid-morning to angle up to the Canadian, Longarm had found himself dozing in the saddle now and then, awakening with start from his short naps and wondering if the chestnut had veered off in the wrong direction.

Old son, you got to settle down and pay attention, he had scolded himself. *You get turned around in country like this and for all you know you might wind up in Jericho or even someplace worse. Now, save your napping till you get to Tascosa. Then you can catch some real shuteye in a real bed.*

After he had gotten within sight of the Canadian, it had been easier for Longarm to stay awake. He still rode near enough to the river to keep it in sight despite its sinuous curves, but far enough away to maintain a reasonably straight course. As he moved farther west, a little variety began to relieve the monotonous, almost featureless sea of low-growing grass.

There was an occasional mesquite patch, and two or three times he saw small bunches of cattle grazing north of the coiling river. At a few spots near the banks there were areas covered by green ground-hugging sand-plum bushes that sprawled out to smother and choke the short, yellowed prairie grass. More rarely there were cottonwood trees standing singly or in small clumps in the moist strip of sand along the riverbank or on one of the narrow, sandy, shoal-like islands that humped a few inches above the surface.

By the time the sun had dropped low enough for its rays to be in his eyes all the time, it seemed to Longarm that he must be riding on an unending journey. He grunted with relief and toed the chestnut to a faster pace when he finally saw the flat tops of buildings breaking the horizon ahead on the opposite bank of the river.

With every yard the chestnut advanced, his view of Tascosa grew clearer. Even with the river still between him and the town he could see evidence of Tascosa's growth that Sara Renfro had mentioned. When he had last seen the town, most of its buildings had been adobe or sod. Now there were several red-brick structures, and many more houses and stores built from lumber.

When Longarm reached Cottonwood Island the trees that gave the little sandbar its name cut off his view of the town. Glancing ahead, he saw that two other major changes had taken place since his last visit. Tascosa's buildings now came almost to the riverbank, and a narrow wooden bridge, just wide enough to accommodate a wagon, had been built across the Canadian a short distance upstream from the mouth of Tascosa Creek.

Well, now, old son, he told himself as he reached the bridge and reined the chestnut onto it, *looks like everybody got tired of trying to get a horse or a team around them quicksand bogs. And I got to admit, it sure makes it easier to get across this damn miserable little river.*

There had been more than enough time during his long, monotonous ride for Longarm to form a strategy of sorts. At the end of the bridge he kept the chestnut moving on the wheel-rutted road to the first row of houses, turned the animal onto Main Street, and rode toward the center of town.

One thing that hadn't changed since his earlier visit was the little creek that rose just north of town and flowed through the full length of Tascosa along one side of a street, predictably named Water Street, to empty into the Canadian. The Howard & McMasters store which was his destination faced Main Street just beyond the creek. He reined the chestnut to a halt in front of the store and went inside. The first person he saw was James McMasters, the man who had been so helpful to Longarm on his last visit.

"Maybe you don't recall me from when I was here a while back, Mr. McMasters," Longarm began.

"I certainly do," the storekeeper broke in. "U. S. Marshal Long. Longarm to your friends, I recall you told me. And, since we made friends when you were here before, I'd rather be called Jim than mister. Welcome back to Tascosa, Longarm."

Longarm looked around the store. It was not crowded, but there were people and clerks within earshot. The storekeeper understood what Longarm's quick survey meant.

"I suppose it will suit you better if we talk in private," he suggested. "Come on, we'll go into my office."

McMasters led Longarm to the back of the store and into a room barely large enough to hold a massive rolltop desk and two or three chairs. Longarm settled down into one of the chairs and lighted a cheroot. "I sure appreciate you taking up your time this way," he told McMasters. "From the looks of the town since I stopped in the last time, you must be doing a right good business."

"None of us in Tascosa has anything to complain about," McMasters nodded. "There's talk we might have a railroad putting tracks through here pretty soon, and if that does happen, I can see the town really booming. But you didn't come here to make a head count on our town, Longarm. Who're you looking for on this trip?"

"A damned outlaw that's being pretty hard for me to catch up with," Longarm replied. "I ain't aiming to impose, but I sorta figured you might've heard about him."

"Well, we got a real rush of ugly customers here in Tascosa after Arrington and his Rangers outfit cleaned out Mobeetie a while back," McMasters said. "But, for the most part, they behave themselves while they're here."

"Do their robbing and looting someplace else, and use your town as a place to rest," Longarm said.

"Well, if we had a town marshal right now, he'd probably roust out any undesirables. As it happens, the sheriff's taken on his job temporarily, until we can find the right man. But I guess we can stand a few for a while without being hurt too bad, as long as they just spend their time in the saloons and red-light district," McMasters went on. "Of course, when somebody like you or some lawman from another town comes after one of them, we don't try to hide them."

Longarm nodded and said, "I'd guess you get a lot of 'em in your store, Jim. But, speaking of your sheriff, I better find him pretty soon and have a little sit-down with him."

"I'm afraid that's not going to be possible," McMasters frowned. "The sheriff's gone down to Clarendon to testify in a case. He'll more than likely be gone a week or so. Anything I can do to help?"

"Not much that comes to mind right now, but thanks for the offer," Longarm told the merchant. "But even if your sheriff was here he might not know the man I'm after, because chances are he'd be travelling under some name

132

like Smith or Jones. Anyhow, the fellow I'm looking for is a young outlaw that calls himself the Kiowa Kid."

McMasters thought for a moment and shook his head. "I don't recall hearing about him. There was a Kiowa Kid on the rampage in these parts quite a while back. Is he the one you're trying to track down?"

"I doubt he's the same one," Longarm replied. "There's been others before that've used that same name. Trouble is, I don't have enough to go by to tell you what this one looks like."

"You must have some kind of description," McMasters said.

"Not much of one, except he's young."

Smiling, the storekeeper said, "Most outlaws are. They're young when they start out and a lot of them are young when they die, too."

"Well, I know about two other Kiowa Kids that's died young, and I don't reckon this one's gonna be much different," Longarm told the merchant. "Except I'm sure going to take this one back all in one piece. The Rangers want him for a killing down along the Red, and the government wants him for robbing the mail and killing a postal clerk."

"He sounds like a bad one," McMasters nodded. "I'll ask around for you quietly, Longarm."

"I'll be staying around here a day or two," Longarm nodded. "There's a few folks I got to ask some questions. I guess you'd know 'em; they're likely customers of yours."

"If they live in Tascosa, they probably are."

"Well, one of 'em is a woman. The only name I got for her is Frenchy. She come here with a man named—"

McMasters broke in before Longarm could finish. "Mickey McCormick," he said.

"That's right," Longarm said.

"You'll find him in his livery stable. It's just across the street, a couple of doors down," McMasters said. Then he shook his head. "I'd be careful asking him about Frenchy, though."

"He's a mite jealous, I take it?"

"That's a mild word, Longarm. And he's got an Irish

133

temper that doesn't take much to trigger it."

"It ain't him I want to talk to as much as I do the woman," Longarm explained. "But I'd imagine I can handle him."

"I'm sure you can," the storekeeper agreed. "How much do you know about him and Frenchy?"

"Not much, except she come over here from Mobeetie with him a while back."

McMasters nodded. "From one of the saloons there. Mickey's running the gambling in Jim East's saloon right down the street from here besides taking care of his livery stable. He used to run the games in a saloon in Mobeetie, I understand."

"Is him and this Frenchy woman married, Jim?"

"Nobody's really sure, but they're living together as though they are."

"Well, I'll keep in mind what you said," Longarm told the merchant. He stood up. "Guess I better get me a room before it's too late. Then I'll look in on that saloon where this McCormick fellow works. I got a horse to stable, but he's likely closed up by now, I'd imagine."

"Oh, he's got a night man, Slats. He'll take your horse in. And I guess you saw the hotel when you rode in. It's just one door down from here, on the corner of Water Street."

"I seen it," Longarm nodded. "Thanks again, Jim. I'll likely drop in on you tomorrow, if you don't mind."

"Come by any time," McMasters replied.

Leaving his horse at the store's hitch rail, Longarm walked the short distance to the Exchange Hotel. He had looked curiously at the stretched-out facade of the low-hung plastered adobe building as he rode past it on his way to the store, and wondered what kind of accommodations it might provide. Taking the doorway below its sign as the main entrance, he opened the screen door and went inside.

A long narrow hall stretched from the door to another door that opened to the outside. The hall was bisected by a corridor that ran the length of the building, and in the square area formed by the intersection stood a table with a dog-eared ledger on it. Before the sound of the closing outer door died away a stooped, white-haired man came out of one of the crossing hallways and stopped beside the table.

"Looking for a room, I guess?" he asked Longarm.

"Sure am. How much you charge?"

"Depends on what you want. Course, this ain't no boarding house, so don't look for no grub. But right catty-corner across from here there's the North Star Cafe. It's right handy, and Jesse Sheets puts out some pretty fair grub."

"Right now, a place to sleep is all I'm looking for," Longarm said. "But I'll keep the cafe in mind. What's your price for a room?"

"Well, we got different kinds of rooms," the oldster replied. He was looking Longarm over with an experienced eye, and when he came to the butt of the Colt in its cross-draw holster he went on, "You can have a single without no door but the one to the hall for fifteen cents a night. If you want a room with another door to the outside, it'll be two bits. If you'll take a double with somebody else, that's fifteen cents, and a double by yourself is half a dollar. No charge for hitching your horse or leaving a wagon setting in the back yard long as you stay."

"I can see where a man might want that extra door," Longarm said thoughtfully. "Reckon it's worth the extra dime."

"Pay in advance, you understand," the clerk said quickly.

"Sure," Longarm nodded, digging out a fifty-cent piece and droping it on the table beside the register. "I'll be here two nights at least, maybe more."

"I'll put you in room seven then. It's got two doors and it's right down at the end of the hall." The clerk pointed out the corridor. "But you'll have to sign the register now. It's a state law, in case you didn't know it."

Longarm bent over the register, dipped his pen beside it into the inkwell, and signed "C. Long" on the page. As he straightened up, he said. "I'll take the key now, if you don't mind. My horse is across the street in front of McMasters's store, so I might as well stop for supper before I walk it to the livery. I'll drop off my saddlebags when I pass by here on my way to look over the town."

"You looking for anything special?"

Longarm shook his head. "Nope. Just looking."

"Well, there's games at most of the saloons. The girls are on the left-hand side, just a block south from here. You can almost always find just what you're looking for here in Tascosa."

Longarm grinned as he replied, "I hope you're right about that."

As he walked back across the deserted street from his horse, Longarm noticed a saloon on the corner diagonally across from the hotel. He angled across to the saloon, tossed off a shot of mediocre rye, then went next door to the restaurant, where he sat at the counter and ate steak and potatoes.

Puffing an after-dinner cheroot, he crossed to unhitch the gelding and led it at a slant back across the street to Mickey McCormick's livery stable, where he arranged for it to be fed and cared for. Slats, the night man, looked thoughtfully at the McClellan saddle and the stirrups with "U. S." branded on their leather toe-shields, but he asked no questions. Carrying his Winchester in one hand and his saddlebags over one shoulder, Longarm returned to the hotel.

Since the evening was still young, he had no urge to hurry. After lighting the kerosene lamp that stood on a small wall shelf at one corner of the bed, he took a look around the tiny rectangular room. It was furnished with a single bed little wider than a cot, and one straight chair.

There was knee-room but little more than required for a man sitting on the side of the bed to keep his knees from bumping the wall. The chair took up most of the space between the foot of the bed and the door that led to the hall. A clothes-hook served in lieu of a wardrobe. The second door opened in the sidewall opposite the bed.

"Well, it sure as hell ain't the Windsor Hotel," Longarm told the empty air as he deposited his saddlebags on the chair and dug the almost-empty bottle of Tom Moore out before sitting down on the side of the bed. Stretching out with a sigh of satisfaction after two long days in the saddle, he took a satisfying swallow of rye before lighting a cheroot and stretching out.

Damned if this ain't almost the end of the line, old son, he mused. *Unless you pick up the trail here, you're pretty much up a stump.*

Longarm smoked his long cheroot down to a stub. Then he rose, and picked up his hat, and went out the side door. Locking it behind him, he tucked the key into his vest pocket and started toward Main Street to look for Jim East's saloon.

Longarm's walk was very short. A glance down Main Street showed him that the south side was lined with residences. On the opposite side, lights spilled from two sets of swinging doors and at the end of the block a lantern above a wide gate indicated the presence of another livery stable. The first set of batwings had "Cattle Exchange Saloon" above them.

Jim East's Saloon proclaimed its identity two doors beyond the Cattle Exchange. Glancing under the batwings, Longarm saw two sets of feet on opposite sides of a long, narrow room. Those on the right were in front of the long brass rail in front of the bar and those on the left were sprawled out, the feet of men sitting in chairs.

Longarm shouldered through the swinging doors and went inside. The men sitting at the round poker table on the left side of the entrance did not look up from their game. Those at the bar flicked their eyes over him with quick, carefully neutral expressions and quickly returned their attention to their drinks or conversations.

Walking to the rear of the bar, Longarm tossed a coin on the mahogany and said, "Maryland rye. If you got some Tom Moore, that's my first choice."

"I think we can oblige you,' the barkeep said. Turning to the backbar, the barkeep ran his eyes along it until he spotted a dusty bottle at one end. He wiped it off on his apron as he returned and picked a glass off the backbar to place in front of Longarm. He uncorked the bottle and asked, "Single or double?"

"Might as well make it a double," Longarm told him.

As the barkeep tilted the bottle to pour, he added, "If you got a spare bottle of that in your storeroom, I'll be glad to buy it off you."

"I think we can oblige you, friend. Rye's not called for very much around here." After Longarm had sipped a swallow of the whiskey the barkeep went on, "New in town, aren't you? At least, I don't recall seeing you before now."

"Oh, I passed through once or twice."

"Always glad to see a new customer," the barkeep said. "I suppose you'll be around a few days, so don't forget us when you feel like a drink next time. Or—" indicating the poker table—"if you feel like trying your luck."

"I just might do that," Longarm said. Then, seeing no real reason for delaying his errand, he went on, "Jim McMasters told me Mickey McCormick's running your games here. Mind pointing him out to me? I'd sorta like to have a word with him."

"That's Mickey at the back side of the table," the barkeep replied.

Longarm nodded. "Thanks. I ain't going to bother him while he's in the middle of playing out a hand."

Mickey McCormick's head was several inches below those of most of the players, indicating that he was short of stature. A fringe of red hair showed below the brim of his pushed-back derby hat. He wore neither coat nor vest, and he had the cuffs of his gleamingly starched white shirt rolled halfway up his forearms. His face was broad, his nose snub above wide lips and a firm jaw.

Sipping his drink, Longarm bided his time. When the hand was played out and he saw McCormick slap the deck on the table and start to stand up, he took the opportunity. Carrying his drink, he strolled to the poker table. Longarm stopped at the side of the gambler. McCormick's head barely reached Longarm's shoulder.

"You wanting to set in?" the gambler asked.

"Maybe. But I got a question to ask you first."

"Ask ahead."

"My name's Long, deputy U. S. marshal outa Denver. I'm looking for a man that's supposed to be in these parts

and a lady in Mobeetie told me I'd oughta talk to your..."
Longarm's hesitation was only momentary. "Your wife, Miz
Frenchy."

He was totally unprepared for the gambler's reaction.

"Damned if you'll talk to my wife!" McCormick growled.

As he began speaking he swivelled in a half-turn and
brought up his right fist in a roundhouse swing aimed at
Longarm's jaw.

Chapter 16

Had Mickey McCormick's hamlike fist landed, Longarm would almost certainly have gotten a broken jaw, but his quick reflexes and superior height saved him. The gambler's first move telegraphed his intention to throw a punch a split second before he began his swing. Longarm drew his head back before McCormick's knuckles fanned past his face.

Longarm realized that if he drew his Colt he would be asking for the kind of trouble that could defeat his mission. As McCormick realized his roundhouse blow had missed and started to pull his arm back for a second swing, Longarm grabbed the gambler's wrist. He gave it a quick hard pull, throwing the angry man off balance.

McCormick resisted, and Longarm found the short man's strength surprising, but he knew the advantage was his as long as he could keep his iron-like grip on his adversary's wrist. He tightened his fingers and kept pulling the arm forward and down until one of the stocky gambler's feet left the floor.

Balancing precariously on one leg, McCormick tried to keep himself from falling by kicking out wildly with his raised foot. It hit the poker table as it came up and the table tilted. It hung balanced precariously on two legs for a moment, then fell forward. Its fall scattered the card players who were still standing beside it and sent cards, glasses, and money cascading to the floor.

Longarm raised his voice and called to the players and to the men rushing from the bar to witness the fight, "You men keep back. There's not going to be no fracas, and what I got to discuss with McCormick is between him and me."

Reluctant, but sensing the authority in Longarm's voice, the onlookers slowly backed away. They clustered along the bar, still watching, but out of earshot now.

McCormick started flailing his free arm, trying to regain control. Longarm's superior reach enabled him to grab the gambler's wildly swinging left hand. He whirled McCormick around. The short man kept struggling to break free, but Longarm's big hands were closed so tightly on his wrists that McCormick could not free them.

"Let go of me, damn you!" he snapped. "If you'll face off man to man, I'll give you a lesson you won't forget in a hurry."

Leaning forward to bring his mouth close to McCormick's ear and keeping his voice level, Longarm replied, "I got an idea you could do just that, McCormick. But I ain't fool enough to let you prove it."

"What the hell are you after?"

"If it makes you feel better, I ain't got a thing against you or your lady, and I don't aim to badger either one of you."

McCormick had stopped trying to free himself. He asked, "How do I know you're telling me the truth?"

Longarm could sense that he was winning now. "I ain't got the name of being a liar, McCormick. Now, I'm going to have to hold on to you till I get your word you'll listen to me peaceful. All I want to do is talk to Miz Frenchy, and if it eases your worry I don't mind a bit talking to both of you together."

Curiosity replaced anger in McCormick's voice as he asked, "Talk about what?"

"About a killer I was sent here to bring in. I got a hunch Miz Frenchy might've run across him in Mobeetie."

"Did you mean what you said a minute ago, about talking to the two of us together?"

"I'm a man of my word, McCormick," Longarm replied. "You can be there when I talk with your lady. But I'll ask you in advance to agree you won't spread what we talk about all over the Texas Panhandle."

"Frenchy and me have both learned how to keep our mouths shut," McCormick said. "And if we do talk with you, I'll guarantee we won't spread around anything you say. Now, will you let go of my arms so we can talk face to face?"

"I'll make you a deal," Longarm offered. "I'll let go of you and I won't fight you if you don't fight me."

"You've got my word," McCormick nodded. "I'll shake on it as soon as you let me go."

Longarm released the gambler's arms. As McCormick turned to face him, he extended his hand. McCormick grasped it in a hand that seemed made of iron, and they pumped arms in a ritual handshake.

McCormick was the first to speak. "Well? You want to tell me what this is all about?"

"Sure," Longarm replied, "but I'd as soon go someplace where we can talk private."

"Then let's just take a little walk," McCormick suggested.

"What about your poker game?"

"To hell with it. I'll close it off."

"Ain't that going to cost you something?"

McCormick shook his head. "Not enough to make any difference. There wasn't anybody sitting who could afford to bet high enough to make the game interesting."

"There's all that money scattered on the floor," Longarm suggested, indicating the strewn coins.

"Give me a minute to get that straightened out," McCormick nodded. "Then Jim East's men can clean up the broken glass along with the rest of the mess."

"Which remind me, I got a little business to tend to," Longarm said. "If I'm in luck, one of them barkeeps has got a bottle of Maryland rye waiting for me."

Longarm paid the barkeep for his bottle of Tom Moore and ordered a shot from the bar bottle. When McCormick joined him, he nodded to the bottle on the bar. "Help yourself."

"No, thanks. I don't have much taste for whiskey any more. The barkeeps in all the saloons where I run my games know to serve me tea. I like to keep my wits about me when I'm dealing; it's part of my edge."

"We might as well go along, then," Longarm said, draining his glass. "I'm paid up here, so let's go to my room over at the Exchange Hotel. It's about as private a place as we can find, I guess."

Longarm led his companion around the corner of the hotel building to the side door. After lighting the lamp, Longarm lifted his saddlebags off the chair and motioned for McCormick to sit down before settling himself on the side of the bed.

"You know, something just popped into my mind," McCormick remarked, a frown puckering his face. "Back there at the saloon, it didn't occur to me that you must be the U. S. marshal they call Longarm. Am I right?"

"Well, folks do call me that sometimes," Longarm admitted. "It's a sorta nickname I picked up."

"I knew it was familiar," McCormick said. "Hell, you're famous! I don't suppose you'd mind if I call you by it, would you? It'd seem a little friendlier. And my friends generally just call me Mickey."

"Fair enough," Longarm nodded. "Now, let's get down to business, Mickey."

"I'm ready as I'll ever be," McCormick agreed. "Who is this fellow you're looking for, and what's Frenchy got to do with him?"

"Now, I never said she had anything to do with him," Longarm said quickly. "She might not ever have set eyes on him, but it's dollars to doughnuts she's heard about him."

"If she had, maybe I have, too. What's his name?"

"He's been travelling under the name of the Kiowa Kid. That ain't his real name, of course. Whoever he is, I got the job of tracking him down and arresting him for murdering a mail clerk a little while back, down along the Red River."

"Oh, hell, Longarm, the Kiowa Kid's been dead for quite a while," McCormick said. "Or at least I heard he was. It seems to me he got shot by some lawman up in Dakota Territory."

"Sure. It was me that shot him," Longarm said. "And that wasn't too long after I'd seen the body of *another* outlaw that called himself the Kiowa Kid, too."

"And you're looking for number three now?" McCormick said.

"You ought've around long enough to know how outlaws is, Mickey," Longarm replied. "This wouldn't be the first time that one of 'em travelled under somebody else's name."

McCormick nodded slowly. "Sure. But whatever name he's going by, you'd have to take him in. You're sure he's in the Panhandle?"

"I ain't certain. About all I got to go by is that some outlaw calling himself that is the man I'm after."

"Hell, Longarm, the Texas Panhandle covers a good-sized chunk of territory. You still haven't told me why you're so sure he's close by."

"I ain't trying to hold nothing back on you, Mickey," Longarm said. "A fellow over in the Indian Nation hinted the Kid might be around Mobeetie or Tascosa."

"He'd have been somebody you trust, I take it?"

"Oh, I wouldn't say I'd believe him about some things, but I do about this one. Not that it makes much difference, but it was Quanah Parker told me that. He'd told the Comanches that he didn't want the Kiowa Kid in Comanche territory, and since the Kiowas and the Comanches are pretty close, I figure Quanah had told the Kiowas he was outlawing him."

"What about Mobeetie?" McCormick asked. "There are still a lot of outlaws in the Canadian brakes over there."

144

"Well, if my friend over there had seen or heard about the Kid being around Mobeetie, she'd've told me."

McCormick studied Longarm's face a moment. "Your friend's a lady, then?"

Longarm nodded. "She used to know your lady when they was both in Mobeetie. She's the one that said I might better talk to Miz Frenchy when I got to Tascosa."

"She's got a name, I guess?"

"Sara Renfro." To save having to answer a follow-up question, he went on, "Miz Frenchy must've known her and her niece, too, when she lived there."

McCormick nodded. "She did. I met Sally myself, but I got the idea Sara'd moved on."

"She left for a while. She's back now, though."

"All right," McCormick said. "I won't object, as long as I'm there when you have your talk with Frenchy."

"I already told you I don't mind that," Longarm replied. "Question now is, when can I talk to her?"

"If you're not too tired to walk a few steps, you can talk to her right now. My house isn't far from here—a block up on Spring Street and two blocks west on Court."

"You're sure it ain't too late?" Longarm asked.

"Frenchy always waits up for me, regardless of how late I am getting home," McCormick said. "She fixes up some kind of little snack, and we sit and talk while we're eating, so we get to bed later than most folks."

"That being the case, we might as well go, then," Longarm nodded.

As McCormick had said, his house was very close. He and Longarm barely had time to exchange a word or two before the gambler pointed to the rectangle of light framed by a window and said, "There we are. I'll just step ahead and tell Frenchy you're with me. I'll leave the door open, so don't bother to knock, just come right on in."

McCormick hurried to the house. Longarm could not see him in the gloom, but soon a second light joined the glow from the window. Longarm reached the house and, taking McCormick at his word, went inside without knocking.

He blinked as the light struck his eyes. Then, as his

vision adjusted to the lighted room, he could make out the details of their features and the recollection of the gambler's jealous explosion in the saloon restrained the involuntary gasp that formed in his throat. Standing beside McCormick was one of the most beautiful women he had ever seen.

Frenchy McCormick stood half a head taller than Mickey. Her face showed no evidence of the years she'd spent as a saloon girl and prostitute. Her creamy skin was unlined, bare of any trace of cosmetics. She wore her glistening black hair swept straight back from her high, smooth forehead, with a cluster of small curls at each side framing her cheeks. The dark dress she wore had a high fitted collar and fell in a straight line to her ankles. It was belted loosely at her waist and fitted tightly enough to show the generous bulge of her breasts.

"Longarm, I'm proud to make you acquainted with my wife," McCormick said. "Frenchy, this is Marshal Long."

Longarm had not yet taken off his hat. He doffed it now and said, "The pleasure's all mine, ma'am. I hope I ain't putting you to no trouble by calling on you so late, but Mickey said it'd be all right."

"Of course it is, Marshal," she replied. Her speech was precise and reminded Longarm of the clipped British accents he had heard from Colorado's influx of English-born ranchers. Frenchy went on, "I'm used to late hours, and I always wait up for Mickey to come home."

"Well, I don't aim to bother you very long," he told her. "I just need to ask you—"

Raising a hand to stop him, Frenchy said, "You don't need to explain or apologize. Mickey and I have a little bite when he gets in, a late supper. Won't you join us? We can talk while we eat."

"Well, that's real nice of you," Longarm said. "I'll be right proud to sit down with you."

Frenchy led the way across the room from the fireplace. "Get a chair for Marshal Long, Mickey," she said. "I'll bring him a plate and we'll start eating. I know you men must be hungry."

When they were seated and had eaten a few bites of

steaming stew and hot biscuits, McCormick said, "I didn't have time to tell you when I got here, Frenchy, but Longarm wants to ask you one or two questions."

"Questions?" Frenchy repeated. A look of alarmed surprise froze her features for a fleeting moment. "What kind of questions, Mickey? Remember what I told you when—"

"Now, it's all right," McCormick broke in. "What Longarm wants to know doesn't have a thing to do with you. He's after an outlaw called the Kiowa Kid, and he thought you might have some idea where he could start looking for him."

Before Frenchy could say anything, Longarm turned to her and said, "I don't aim to bother you, Miz Frenchy, but Sara Renfro over in Mobeetie said you might've heard something that'd give me a lead."

"You know Sara?" Frenchy asked.

"Oh, sure," Longarm nodded. "We got acquainted a while back when I was in Mobeetie on a case. I didn't reckon it'd do any harm for me to look you up."

Frenchy sat silently for a moment, then said slowly, "Sara knows that I put my old life behind me when I came here with Mickey. But I've been away from Mobeetie such a long time that I don't . . . well, that's not important. I remember a Kiowa Kid was there at one time, but I never did know him. I think he got killed somewhere up in Dakota Territory quite some time ago."

McCormick broke in. "I guess that answers your question, Longarm. Now, let's just forget about outlaws and all that and enjoy our supper."

147

Chapter 17

After the long days on horseback, nights of sleeping between blankets on the hard prairie soil, and the late-night visit with Mickey and Frenchy McCormick, Longarm slept past sunrise in his room at the Exchange Hotel. As usual, he woke fully alert and had a healthy swallow of Tom Moore before lighting a cheroot and stretching out on his rumpled bed to smoke it while he considered the day ahead.

Looks like you're up shit creek without no paddle, old son, he told himself.

Before his cigar had been smoked to a stub, Longarm's stomach was reminding him that is was long past his usual breakfast time. He rose and dressed and had a final sip from his bottle, and went out the side door. Main Street was just beginning to come to life, and aside from clerks opening the shutters of two or three of the establishments there was no one in sight.

Crossing the street, he went on to the restaurant where he had had supper the previous evening.

He made a quick job of breakfast and started across Main

Street back to the hotel when a man hailed him from across the street.

"Good morning, Marshal! Hope you slept well!"

Longarm recognized James McMasters. "Morning, Mr. McMasters. If it ain't too early to have a drink, I'll buy you one over there at the Cattle Exchange Saloon."

"Thanks, but you guessed right," McMasters replied. "It is early in the day for me. But there's always a pot of coffee ready in the store by now. If you'll settle for that, suppose you come join me."

Longarm angled over to the corner where McMasters stood waiting.

"I'm curious to know if you learned anything useful from Frenchy McCormick last night," the merchant said as they went into his small private office.

"Not much of anything," Longarm replied as he sat down. "It was just like butting up against a brick wall."

"I was afraid that'd be the case," McMasters said. "You may not know it, but the ladies in town who don't have much to do besides gossip say that after Mickey brought Frenchy here from Mobeetie she swore not to say anything at all about her past."

"Well, she didn't seem to balk too much after Mickey told her it was all right for her to talk to me. The trouble was, she didn't know much. But I'll give her this, she sure acted like a lady."

"Oh, Frenchy didn't grow up in a gutter, the way so many saloon women did. She's supposed to have come from a good family and been educated in a convent in Europe somewhere—France, the story has it—and run away with a man that brought her to this country and then deserted her."

"All of that don't help me none," Longarm commented. "I wasn't looking for her to come right out and tell me where I could find the Kiowa Kid. I got so little to go on that I guess I sorta over-hoped."

For a moment they sat without speaking. Then McMasters said slowly, "Longarm, if you really think you're going to need some help finding this Kiowa Kid, there's one man here who might be able to give you a hand."

"A lawman that's handed over his badge and hung up his guns?"

McMasters shook his head. "No. The man that runs our newspaper. His name's Rudolph."

"Rudolph what?"

"That's his last name. He won't give out what his initials stand for. They're C. F., but I guess they stand for something outlandish, so everybody calls him Rudy."

Longarm said, "I guess I run up against as many newspaper people as most anybody has, but I never got much help from one of 'em. What gives you the idea this Rudolph fellow could give me a hand?"

"Well, it's just an idea, Longarm. Call it a hunch. You just said you had one newspaperman help you close a case."

"I wasn't talking about a man, Jim. It was a little half-pint woman that called herself Nellie Bly, and she give me a hand closing a case over in the Nation. Tell me about this Rudolph fellow. One thing sure, I got lots of time to listen."

"Well, Rudy covers a lot of ground when he's picking up news. He's got a way of getting people to open up when they're talking to him. He goes out to the ranches all the time, so he might've heard something a hand let drop that wouldn't mean much to him or me, but might to you."

"I hadn't looked at it that way, Jim," Longarm said. "Might be you're right. I guess since I'm scratching at straws, I might as well go scratch at a good one." He stood up. "Where'll I find this Rudolph fellow?"

"Just go outside and walk a block down Spring, then turn to your right and go another block on First Street. The newspaper office is on the left-hand corner."

"Thanks," Longarm said.

Out on the street, the sunshine warm now, Longarm strolled without hurrying to the building down the block where he saw a sign, *The Tascosa Pioneer*. The door was open, and when he went in he found the building deserted except for a man in the rear setting type.

"I don't guess Mr. Rudolph's around?" he called.

"I just guess he is," the compositor replied. "You're

looking at him. And who might you be? I don't recall seeing you around Tascosa before."

"My name's Long, Mr. Rudolph. Deputy U. S. marshal outa the Denver office. Mr. McMasters said you're a man I might better talk to."

"If Jim McMasters sent you here, I'll listen with both ears."

"Well, now, I don't wanta keep you from your work."

"Never too busy to listen," Rudolph said. "When a man's been at a job as long as I have this one, he gets to where he can talk and listen and set a stick of type all at the same time." He tilted his head to look at Longarm from below the rim of the green visor he was wearing. "Go ahead and tell me what's on your mind, Marshal Long." He paused and his brow crinkled. "Wait a minute. It didn't hit me until now. Are you by any chance the U. S. marshal they call Longarm?"

"Folks sorta hung that on me," Longarm nodded.

"Why, I'll be! I'd like to know what's brought you to Tascosa, Longarm. My nose for news tells me there's a story in it, and the *Pioneer* can always use a good local yarn."

"Well, now, I didn't come in just to get my name in the paper," Longarm said. "Matter of fact, I'd as soon you didn't put nothing in your paper about me being in town. It might spook off the man I'm trying to find."

"I wouldn't want to interfere with your work," Rudolph said quickly. "I'll keep your name out of the paper until you've found your man."

"I appreciate that."

Rudolph added quickly, "But I'll expect you to let me be the first to know when you've run him down."

"I'll sure be glad to do that," Longarm said. "Only right now it looks like you might have to wait longer than either one of us would like."

"I take that to mean you don't have much hope of finding him?"

"I didn't say that," Longarm replied. "I got a real strong hunch he's someplace inside of a day's ride from Tascosa.

Trouble is, there's so many places a man on the dodge can hide around here, all the valleys and arroyos and caves."

"It's torn-up country, all right," Rudolph agreed. "But where do I fit into your plan, if you've got one?"

"Well, you ride out regular to the big ranches, Jim says. I imagine you'd talk to the hands?"

"Of course," the newspaperman nodded.

"So you'd hear a lot of range gossip," Longarm went on. "They'd likely mention if they've seen strange riders, signs of camps, things like that."

"I'd say I hear more than most people do," Rudolph agreed. "The men on the spreads know me by now. They talk pretty freely about anything out of the ordinary."

"Have any of 'em said anything about strange camps, maybe a steer rustled by somebody who might not feel safe coming into town to buy victuals?"

Rudolph shook his head. "Not lately. It's been a month or more since I recall any of the range riders mentioning that they ran into a strange camp. But they tracked down the people that had made it and it turned out to be a bunch of immigrants who'd gotten lost."

Longarm kept himself from showing his disappointment. "Well, I thank you for your time, Mr. Rudolph. If your hear anything that might point me in the right way, I'd appreciate you letting me know. I'm staying at the Exchange Hotel."

"I'll keep it in mind," Rudolph promised.

Longarm turned and started for the door. He was still a step or two away from it when the newspaperman's call stopped him and brought him back.

"Longarm!" Rudolph said. "Hold on a minute. I might have an idea that'd help you."

"I'm sure wide open to new ideas," Longarm told him.

"Have you ever thought about advertising?"

His face crinkled into a question, Longarm repeated, "Advertising?" He shook his head. "I ain't got anything to sell, Mr. Rudolph. I'm looking for information, not customers, like a storekeeper would be."

"Look at it this way," Rudolph suggested. "Anybody who has information that might help you is a customer."

After a moment's thought, Longarm nodded slowly. "Well, I reckon you got a point, even if it does stretch things some."

"Now, the *Pioneer* goes to a lot of people outside of Tascosa, all the ranches and a lot of the sodbusters that've taken up land hereabouts," Rudolph went on. "Why, just a few weeks ago we increased our press run. We're putting out more than two hundred copies a week!"

Longarm nodded slowly. "I see what you're getting at, Mr. Rudolph, only I don't quite figure exactly what you got in mind. I wouldn't imagine that if the Kiowa Kid seen a story saying I was in town looking for him, he'd march in and give himself up. He'd be more likely to get out as fast as he could."

"That's not at all what I was thinking about," the newspaperman said. "Wherever this man is hiding, somebody knows who he is. I'd guess that when he gets wind of you being here he'll start running again."

"I figure that's about right," Longarm agreed.

"He'd be nervous and in a hurry," Rudolph went on. "And an outlaw running under those conditions will leave a pretty broad trail. I'm sure you're capable of following it."

"I'd imagine so," Longarm nodded. "Only I still don't see how I'm going to get onto his trail in the first place."

"Well..." Rudolph began, then fell silent, frowning. "You'd have to depend on somebody who knew about this outlaw coming to you and giving you a place where you could start after him," Rudolph said at last. "And they'd expect something for their trouble. I'd suggest offering a reward to anybody who brought you information."

"Mr. Rudolph, if you had any idea how long it takes for the U. S. government to turn loose of money for a reward—"

Rudolph didn't wait for Longarm to continue. He broke in, "I understand that. I was thinking of the *Pioneer* offering the reward."

"I'll admit you make it sound right easy," Longarm said thoughtfully. "Except I got one question to put to you. When does your next paper come out?"

"On Friday."

"And this ain't but Monday," Longarm went on. "If the Kiowa Kid's holed up someplace close by, and he got wind of what we're aiming to do, he'd hightail it and cover his trail so I might not even get in spitting distance of him."

Rudolph was silent for a moment. Then he nodded. "You've got a point there, all right." His brows knitted, he went on slowly, "I'll tell you what, Longarm. There's hardly a day goes by without a man coming in from the big spreads hereabouts to pick up the mail, get something for the cook, or just to have a drink and raise a bit of hell. Suppose I print up a bunch of posters offering a reward and put them into all the stores and saloons in town?"

"Figuring that whoever sees a poster will sorta spread the news?" Longarm nodded. "Now, that just might work."

Rudolph went on, "Maybe we can even improve on it. The mail wagon's due in from the west late today. It goes as far as Mobeetie, and the driver swings off the road to stop at some of the big spreads between here and there. I can give him a few posters to drop off on the way."

Longarm was getting into the spirit of things now. He said, "I'd imagine Jim McMasters would help out some. He's likely to have some deliveries going out to the ranches today and tomorrow. And there's Mickey McCormick. I'd guess there's men from other towns coming into his livery stable."

"You're in favor of it, I see."

"Sure I am! Why, them posters can cover ten times as much ground as I could myself."

"It might not get you close to the man you're after, though. Once he gets wind of them, he's likely to start moving."

"That don't bother me for a minute, Mr. Rudolph. Once that Kiowa Kid gets spooked out, he'll take off running, and I'll gamble I can pick up his tracks and catch up with him." Longarm stopped suddenly and shook his head. "Except we left a big hole to the west of here. If he runs that way, I might have some trouble."

"There's not all that much to the west," Rudolph said.

"If the posters go out the way we've planned, they'll get to the only spreads of any size in that direction."

"I don't guess there's any towns that way?"

"Just one. Hayes is about twelves miles west, on the army supply road."

"If it ain't but twelve miles, I can ride that way. On the army road I can be there and back before midnight if I get going before noon. But ain't there nothing to the south?"

Rudolph shook his head. "Not a thing short of a three-day ride. Oh, there's Ragtown, down on a draw about thirty miles, but it's just a few soddies and a cabin or two."

"How long's it going to take to get them posters printed up?" Longarm asked.

"What I'm doing now can wait," Rudolph told him. "I can have a hundred posters off the press in a hour."

Longarm looked around the bare building. "All by yourself?"

"I'll be using big block type," Rudolph replied. "I set it in the form instead of a stick and justify as I go."

"Well, I don't savvy printers' lingo, but if you say you can, I'll take your word. If you don't mind, I'll sorta hang around in case you need an extra hand."

While Longarm watched, Rudolph worked for the next hour like a demon. Longarm picked a spot far enough from the press to be out of the way. A few minutes before the time the newspaperman had promised, he brought the stack of posters to Longarm and held one up. Longarm read the glaring words:

REWARD
FOR INFORMATION
ABOUT OUTLAW CALLED
THE KIOWA KID
BRING TO U. S. MARSHAL
C. LONG
AT *TASCOSA PIONEER*

"That sure looks fine," Longarm told Rudolph. "Now all we got to do it put 'em where they'll do the most good."

Chapter 18

"You think you've put out enough bait, Longarm?" Jim McMasters asked as they sat puffing on their cigars. The dishes from their supper still sat on the table, pushed back from the edge. After his return from Hayes, Longarm had been glad enough to accept the merchant's invitation to dine, and McMasters's cook had served them a steaming heap of antelope steaks from a carcass traded at the store for ammunition by a market hunter.

"Well, if we didn't it wasn't because we overlooked any place close enough to reach in the time we had. Course, I ain't such a much at fishing, Jim. When I'm out on a case, I'll wait at a stakeout till hell freezes over, but if the fish don't start biting right after I throw in my bait, I get tired of waiting and just pull out my line and quit cold.'"

"I'm inclined to be that way myself," the merchant nodded. "But, from what Rudolph told me when he looked in at the store just before you got back, you got rid of a lot of your posters today."

"You know, I had a lot of time to think about them signs

156

while I was riding down to Hayes and back. Even if the Kiowa Kid don't see one himself, some of the outlaws around here might've, and a lot of them renegades will turn against their own kind without batting an eye if there's enough in it for 'em."

"Give it a couple of days to work," McMasters advised. "I feel about as optimistic as you do. I sure hope you've thrown a big enough loop to grab the man you're after."

"Well, we'll know by this time tomorrow or the next day," Longarm said. He pushed away from the table and stood up. "I sure thank you for the supper, Jim. That cook of yours done herself proud. But it's about time for me to get some shuteye, now. I told Mr. Rudolph I'd be down at his office first thing in the morning."

Back at the Exchange Hotel, Longarm wasted little time in stripping off his clothes and falling into bed. He woke once some time during the night when a crowd of boisterous cowhands passed by on the street outside his room, singing and joshing one another at the tops of their voices, then immediately went back to sleep and did not open his eyes until the room was filled with dawn light.

Longarm started dressing. Within three minutes he was ready to leave. As an afterthought, he picked up the Winchester that stood in a corner of his room and started for Jesse Sheets's North Star Restaurant.

Sitting at the counter, he finished his bacon and eggs and soft-fried potatoes and swallowed what was left of his second cup of black coffee. Picking up his Winchester, he moved to the front of the L-shaped counter near the door to pay his bill. A pair of cowhands, obviously nursing hangovers from the night before, were arguing over which of them had invited the other to breakfast and who was supposed to settle for their meal.

Standing behind them waiting his turn to step up to the till, Longarm caught a glimpse of himself in the foot-square mirror that hung on the wall. Instinctively, his hand went to his chin to finger his three-day growth of beard.

You got to find a barbershop, old son, he told himself. *If Billy Vail was to see you now he'd boot you outa his office and tell you to come back when you looked like one of his men and not some saddle tramp just getting over a four-day spree.*

As he shelled out the money for his breakfast, Longarm asked the proprietor, "Mind telling me where the barbershop's at? I ain't had time to do much looking around since I got to town."

"Well, the barber that we had here closed up shop and moved away a couple of months ago, Marshal Long," the restaurant owner replied.

Though Longarm had been in the cafe only once, he was not surprised to be addressed by his name. He'd been in enough small Western towns to know that a stranger's arrival became common knowledge within a matter of hours, if not minutes.

"I guess I'm just going to have to get used to this brush I'm sprouting, then," he remarked.

"Well, most of us went back to shaving at home," the cafe owner said, "but just lately Mickey McCormick's livery man, Slats, has opened up a sort of halfway barbershop at Mickey's stable. I haven't had to have him shave me yet, but he did a pretty good job on my hair, even if all he had to use was some horse clippers."

"Seeing as it's right next door, I'll just step over and give him a try. These whiskers are starting to itch."

Passing the metallic banging and deep crimson glow that came from the blacksmith shop between the restaurant and the livery stable, Longarm turned in at the wide gate. There were a few horses and mules clomping around on the well-beaten earth of the yard, but Slats was nowhere to be seen. Longarm started toward the stable, which stretched across the back of the pole-fenced yard, but before he'd taken more than half-dozen steps he saw Slats come out of the stable and start toward him, swinging a tin bucket in one hand.

"You come for your nag, Marshal?" he asked. "I'll have him ready for you in about two minutes, if you're heading out."

"No, that ain't why I'm here," Longarm answered. "I hear you can shave a man without chopping his gullet open,

158

so I'm looking for you to shave me."

"Why, sure." Slats lifted the bucket. "I even got hot water, so you won't have to wait. Had to heat a couple of buckets to purge a hoss that's got a bad load of pinworms, and there's enough left to shave you with."

"I'll just ask one thing of you," Longarm said. He carried his forefinger along one side of his steerhorn moustache and gave the tip a little twirl. "Don't go hacking at my moustache."

"Now, you don't need to worry, Marshal Long," the stableman replied. "I learned a long time ago not to mess with a man's face-trim. Just step on in the office, now, and I'll have that brush of yours cleared away in a jiffy."

Seated in a straight chair in the center of the little ten-foot-square livery-stable office, a horse blanket spread over his shoulders for a barber-cloth, Longarm turned and twisted and tilted his head at the liveryman's direction while his cheeks and jaws were shaved with surprising skill.

"Where'd you learn how to shave, Slats?" Longarm asked as the job neared completion.

"Why, I rode with the Seventy-seventh Cavalry for two hitches," Slats replied. "One time while we was in the field chasing a pack of renegade Apaches our hosses had a spell of sore-tail. The only way we could clear it up was to keep their asses shaved clean. Taken three months to get 'em cured, and by then I was a pretty fair hand with a razor."

Longarm chuckled. "And I guess you've shaved a few more horses' asses since then."

"I sure have, only they've been the two-legged kind." Slats put his razor aside and held the bucket of warm water where Longarm could reach it. "You c'n sorta rinse off now. I ain't got anything for you to dry with, but—"

"I'll use my bandana, thanks," he said, pulling it from his hip pocket and wiping his face. "How much do I owe you?"

"I reckon a dime's about right," Slats replied. He cocked his head as he took the coin Longarm handed him. "You do look some better, Marshal."

"I feel better, too." Longarm picked up his rifle and

started for the door. "I better hyper on over to the newspaper office now. Mr. Rudolph's going to be wondering what happened to me. I told him I'd be on hand if somebody come in about that flyer we put out yesterday."

"Sure. Mickey brought me one to put up here, but I ain't got around to tacking it up yet," Slats nodded.

Stopping in the doorway, Longarm turned back and said, "It sure ain't going to do no good unless folks can see it."

"Now you've reminded me, I'll put it up today, for sure," Slats said.

"You do that," Longarm nodded. He stepped down to the path in front of the door just as a rifle barked. Its slug tore into the wooden doorjamb where his head had been framed a second before.

After the hidden gunman's first shot missed its target, the instinctive reactions finely honed by years of encounters with desperate criminals saved Longarm's life. While walking the few steps from the restaurant to his destination, he had passed a small slit of open space between the livery office and the blacksmith shop next door. As Longarm hit the ground, the position of the small opening flashed back into his mind. Too wise to give his would-be killer an easy target, he began rolling to it.

Before he reached the opening, the hidden sniper fired again. This time the bullet raised a puff of dust as it thunked into the ground only inches from Longarm's moving body. This second near-miss added impetus to Longarm's moves, and before the sniper had time for a follow-up shot, Longarm had snaked into the narrow opening and was shielded between the two buildings.

Without breaking the rhythm of his movements, Longarm came to his feet. The little crevice was barely wide enough to accommodate his broad shoulders, but Longarm squeezed them together and started edging toward the street. He had placed the position of his unknown attacker with the sniper's second shot, and knew that the man was shooting from the shelter of the last building on the block.

As he struggled to edge forward in the narrow space Longarm realized at once that with the sniper on his right

160

the only way he could get off a shot without stepping into the street and exposing himself fully would be to shoulder his rifle on his left. He had brought up his Winchester when he got to his feet, and as he moved cautiously forward he shifted hands on the Winchester in preparation for a quick shot.

Holding the rifle ready, Longarm inched to the end of the opening. He braced himself on the wall of the blacksmith shop, then hunkered down before peering out. His move placed his head only a yard or so from the ground, far below the level where the sniper would expect it to be.

Within the limited range of his vision, Longarm saw that the street was deserted, but he could hear the slamming of doors from the stores on both sides of the street and a babble of excited voices. His careful scrutiny of the buildings he could see, from the corner of McMasters' store to the Shelton Drug Store sign at the end of the block, showed people running out of the store buildings, but none of them was carrying a rifle.

Longarm took off his hat and put it on the muzzle of his Winchester. An inch at a time, he extended the hat from the slit, holding it at waist level. It drew no fire, so he raised the weapon's muzzle to a height where his head would normally appear when he peeked out. He held it there for several moments, but still his bait did not bring a bullet.

That means the son of a bitch has broke cover and moved, old son, Longarm told himself. *Now, there's most likely no cover close to that last building, so he's either running away or he's dodging along the street to see if he can get a head-on shot. Now, anybody that'd try to shoot a man down in broad open daylight in the middle of town has got guts enough or is fool enough to keep on trying. Chances are he's heading this way along that side street, and if you're figuring right, the smart thing for you to do is back up and try to catch him before he sees you.*

Even before he had reached his decision, Longarm was turning sideways to edge along the narrow space to its end at the rear corner of the livery office. He stopped again before leaving his place of concealment and dropped flat before peering out across the livery stable yards. Ahead and to his right the stables stood, a horse trough at their far end. The animals that had been in the yard had clustered beyond the trough in the space between the stables and the fence at their far end and were milling nervously.

"Looks like that's the answer," Longarm muttered aloud. "If it was me trying to get at a man in my situation, I'd think ahead, just like that son of a bitch did. He seen right away that I wasn't apt to come out from the other end of that crack, and sure as God made little green apples he's hunkered down back of that watering trough waiting for me to show."

By turning back and making his way to the rear of the livery office, Longarm had reversed the awkward position he'd been in when he was at the end opening into the street. Now he could get his Winchester on his right shoulder, and he did so, holding the muzzle down parallel to his body, his finger ready on the trigger.

In one swift move he stepped out, brought up the rifle, and sent a slug singing into the watering trough. The bullet thunked into the wooden side of the tank, plowed through the boards, and sent water shooting up in a sheet. Through the haze of rising water Longarm saw his enemy stand up.

With the skill acquired in many equally precarious situations, he aimed well. Through the haze of the falling water he sent a bullet on its way. As the mist of water cleared he saw a man standing swaying in back of the trough, a rifle shouldered.

Longarm fired again before noticing that the other man was already crumpling. In such a situation, Longarm had proved the accuracy of his shooting many times. The second slug took the swaying man in the chest and tore through his heart, sending him staggering back a few paces before he toppled to the ground and lay motionless.

As he started walking carefully toward the sprawled form lying facedown on the hoof-pocked earth of the livery yard, Longarm kept his Winchester ready to bring up instantly, his finger still on the trigger. The stillness that had settled over the scene during the first few seconds after the rifle-fire ended was being broken now by excited voices coming from the direction of Main Street.

By the time Longarm reached the corpse, men were pouring into the livery yard from the street. Jim McMasters was among the first to reach Longarm's side.

"Is that the Kiowa Kid?" he asked.

"I ain't had time to look, Jim," Longarm replied. "I sure hope it ain't, because my chief told me to bring him back all in one piece."

"You had to kill him in self-defense," McMasters protested. "Surely he won't blame you for that."

"I don't imagine he'd bear down too hard, the way things has worked out," Longarm agreed. "But before I start borrowing trouble, I better take a look at this fellow and see who he is. Will it bother you to give me a hand turning him face up?"

McMasters shook his head. "Not a bit. This wouldn't be the first corpse I've handled."

Bending over the body, Longarm and the storekeeper turned it face upward. After looking at the dead man's face closely, Longarm said, "It ain't the Kiowa Kid, Jim. I knew this fellow a long time before the Kid popped up. His name's Zaragosa, or it was when I bumped up against him. He's a renegade from the Mexican *Rurales*. I had a pretty bad run-in with him down along the Rio Grande a few years back."

"I recognize him, too, but I don't recall ever hearing his name," McMasters nodded. "He's been in and out of Tascosa for a couple of years that I know of. I never did think of him as a killer, though."

"You scratch one of them *Rurales*, you'll find a killer most of the time. They don't have laws like ours in Mexico."

"I suppose," McMasters nodded. "Well, it looks like the town's going to have to bury him—not that he's the first one, and likely he won't be the last. You might as well go about your business, Longarm. I'm on the town council. I can take care of what's necessary."

A clump of curious spectators were pushing close now, staring at the corpse. There was a stirring at the back of the group. Longarm and McMasters turned to look just as Rudolph, the newspaper editor, pushed through. He glanced at the sprawled body for a moment and turned to Longarm and the storekeeper.

"Is that the man you're after?" he asked Longarm.

"No, he ain't, Mr. Rudolph," Longarm replied. "I know him, or did. We crossed paths down in Mexico a few years back, and he come out second-best. I guess he just seen me sometime yesterday and decided to even up scores."

"I've told Longarm the town will take care of putting him away," McMasters volunteered. "I guess you'll be wanting to write it up for the *Pioneer*, won't you?"

"Why, sure," Rudolph replied. "Ordinarily, it wouldn't draw more than a half-stick, but with Marshal Long involved, it'll make a pretty fair story."

McMasters said, "I'll leave that to you and Longarm, then. If you'll excuse me, I've got to pick three or four men out of this crowd here to haul this fellow up to Boot Hill."

"And we'd better get over to the *Pioneer* office," the editor told Longarm. "I know it's early in the day, but I've got a lot of type to set if I'm going to have a paper this week. You can tell me how this all came about and I'll set it up first thing and get it out of the way."

"Sure," Longarm nodded. "But let's walk on down Main Street, if you don't mind. I'd like to stop in at that saloon I found last night where they got my favorite whiskey. I know it's a mite early, but I sorta feel like I been up a long time, and a swallow of Tom Moore would go down mighty good about now."

164

Chapter 19

"Like I said, I'll wait it out another day or maybe two," Longarm told Rudolph. "But I ain't real tickled just setting on my butt waiting for a man I'm after to come look me up."

"Now, if you'll remember, I didn't say the Kiowa Kid himself was going to walk into the *Pioneer* office and surrender to you," Rudolph reminded him.

"Oh, I ain't making out you said anything like that, Rudy," Longarm protested. "Outlaws ain't built that way. I oughta know, because I've run down more'n one."

Longarm and the *Pioneer* editor were sitting at supper in the restaurant, where they'd moved after having a drink in the saloon next door. It had been a long day for both of them, but Longarm had felt its drag more than Rudolph. He'd had nothing to do except sit and wait, while the editor had been busy with his regular work.

"Give that poster time to circulate," the editor advised. "It's just now getting handed around."

"Sure. I ain't given up on it," Longarm assured his com-

165

panion. "I seen it work; it skunked out that Mexican renegade, not that I'd give any thought it would."

"More people will see it every day it circulates," Rudolph pointed out encouragingly.

"I ain't a man that gives up on much of anything," Longarm replied, "but if he don't see that poster and I don't start after him, he's gonna put more space between me and him than I like to think about." He drained his glass and put it back on the table, then stood up. "It's time for me to turn in, Rudy. I'll be around to the newspaper office first thing in the morning."

Back in his room at the Exchange Hotel, Longarm poured a nightcap and sipped at it while making the bedtime preparations that were his regular routine. He hadn't yet stretched out comfortably before a light tapping sounded on the outside door.

Picking up the Colt, he moved to the door, his bare feet silent on the warped floorboards. As he started toward the door the tapping was repeated. Standing to one side of the thin door panels, Longarm asked, "Who is it?"

"Longarm?" a woman's voice replied. "Let me in, please."

There was something familiar about the voice, but Longarm could not put a name or a face to it, and aside from Frenchy McCormick he'd met no women in Tascosa. "You mind telling me your name before I open up?" he asked.

"It's Ellen, Longarm. Ellen Briscoe."

His tension relaxed instantly and Longarm opened the door. His unexpected visitor slipped inside and he closed and locked the door behind her.

"Don't light the lamp again," she said, moving closer to him. "We've never missed the light before."

Longarm eyes had adjusted to the darkness by now and when Ellen turned her face up he bent to kiss her. When lack of breath ended their embrace she said, "I was wondering if I'd forgotten what your kisses do to me. I haven't."

"I couldn't fault you if you'd forgot, Ellen," Longarm said. "It's been a while."

"Too long," she replied.

"How'd you find out I was..." Longarm began, then

stopped and went on, "Them posters, of course."

"Yes. One of the hands rode over here yesterday to pick up the mail, and brought back your poster with it. I couldn't get away last night, no matter how much I wanted to, but I didn't waste any time leaving today, and in a little place like this it wasn't much of a trick to find out where you were staying."

"I take that as a real compliment, Ellen," Longarm said. "You remembering me all the time since I was here last." Then he added hurriedly, "Not that I've forgot you. When I got to the Canadian on my way here I recalled how we run into each other and wondered was you still at your brother-in-law's ranch."

"You saved me from more than quicksand when you saw how badly I was bogged down," she told him. "But you spoiled me for any other man when I came to your room that night."

"Well, I remember a lot more'n the quicksand, too," Longarm told her.

"Now you're flattering me," Ellen said, a smile in her voice. "But I didn't ride all the way here just to swap compliments." She dropped her hand to Longarm's thigh and found his recumbent shaft. Feeling it through the cloth of his balbriggans she went on, "You're not ready as I am, of course. I've been thinking about you since I left the ranch. But I'm sure you'll be ready by the time you get my clothes off, and now that I've seen you I just can't wait any longer."

As Ellen spoke she was levering off her calf-length boots. She stood up and Longarm helped her out of her riding jacket and blouse. When she leaned on him for balance while dropping her split skirt and pantalettes he found her big soft breasts with his hands and began caressing them, rubbing their protruding tips.

Ellen's breath was coming faster when she stood naked in front of Longarm and stripped away his balbriggans. His erection rose free when his underwear dropped.

Longarm bent to kiss her. As their lips pulsed together and their tongues entwined, Ellen pressed close to Longarm's chest and began twisting her torso to rub the tips of her breasts against the wiry mat of hair on his chest. Ellen was breathing in quick, short gasps when at last their lips parted; Longarm lifted her and took a step toward the bed.

Longarm kept up a steady pace, slow, deliberate penetrations in an easy, even rhythm, and Ellen's soft sighs grew loud. When the sighs became short, wordless exclamations and he felt her body beginning to tremble he speeded up. Ellen responded almost at once. Her hips and torso began writhing in rhythm with his thrusts, and when she broke the rhythm and began squirming, he closed his hands around her hips and began stroking faster.

Suddenly Ellen's voice filed the little room with a loud, sobbing scream that hung quivering in the air. Her back arched into a bow. Her body was shaking franatically, and her loud cries reached a peak as her hips twisted in a final spasm. Longarm held them firmly and thrust in one final deep drive that brought a last throaty yell in response before her muscles relaxed, her body sagged, and her cries subsided to small ecstatic moans.

"I'm glad you don't give up quick," she said. "I never have felt the way I do now. I'm too tired to keep going, but I don't want to stop."

"We don't have to stop now," Longarm told her. He thrust slowly but deeply.

"Ohh!" Ellen moaned throatily. "Do that again, Longarm!"

Longarm brought his hips forward once more, and when Ellen made no reply except a happy sigh, he resumed the slow-paced stroking that had marked the beginning of their encounter. Life came back to Ellen's body almost at once. Soon she was responding to Longarm's deep drives with as much enthusiasm as he was showing with his increasingly fast pounding.

She rose quickly to another spasm of writhing, shrieking ecstasy, and Longarm rose with her this time. He carried her to her peak and joined her when she reached it, his legs braced and his muscles taut.

Groping in his vest pocket, Longarm found a cigar and a match and lighted up. To their eyes, conditioned to almost

168

total darkness, the glow of the cheroot's tip made the little room as bright as though he had lighted the lamp.

Ellen snuggled up to Longarm and put her head on his shoulder. "I don't suppose you can stay any longer than you did the last time," she said. Before Longarm could reply she went on, "I'm running the ranch now. Bob and Annie have gone to Europe for a year or two. My foreman quit last week, and I'm looking for a new one. If you'd take the job we could spend every night like this."

"Now, Ellen, you know I couldn't stand to give up my work," Longarm replied, his voice gentle. "I'm real flattered that you'd want me, but ranching just ain't my style. I found that out when I tried it before I got on the marshal's force."

"I knew that's what you were going to say," Ellen sighed. "You ain't mad, then?"

"Of course not, Longarm." Ellen lifted herself to kiss him, but made no effort to prolong the kiss. She lay back and went on, "I made up my mind not to ask you more than once." Her hand slid down Longarm's body and closed over his limp shaft. "But I didn't come here just to offer you a job, and once isn't enough for what I really want."

"It ain't for me, either," Longarm agreed as he stubbed out his cigar. "And I aim to make the most of what time we got now, just the same as you do."

His chair propped up against the partition formed by the chest-high type cases that stretched across the center of the *Tascosa Pioneer* office, Longarm leaned back with his eyes closed, resting after his sleepless night.

Ellen Briscoe had ridden away in the soft pre-dawn light, and though Longarm was a bit ragged after his exertions he hadn't felt like going back to a lonely bed. Dressing quickly, he had walked to the restaurant and had breakfast an hour earlier than usual. Fully awake by then, he had moved the short distance down Main Street to Jim East's Saloon and sat sipping Tom Moore until he judged it was time for the *Pioneer* office to open.

"You're out early today," Rudolph had greeted him. "But I always say the early morning's the best time of day."

"Most of the time I wouldn't argue you about that," Longarm replied. "But I got an awful itch today to get moving again, Rudy. I don't think them posters is going to bring in the Kiowa Kid, no more'n a duck call would bring in a deer."

"Let's just settle down and be patient and see what the day brings," Rudolph advised. "Now, I've got type to set, so you just make yourself at home while I go to work."

Longarm had been hanging on the fine line between wakefulness and slumber when Rudolph's hand closed on his shoulder. He was wide awake at once. "What's wrong?" he asked the editor.

"Maybe nothing," Rudolph replied, his voice low. "But in the last five minutes I've heard a noise outside two or three times which gives me an idea somebody might be prowling around out there."

"Where'd you hear it first?"

"Up at the front corner of the building, then along the street side, and just then I heard something at the back."

Longarm glanced around the long, rectangular room. The rows of double-hung windows that broke the walls, four on each side of the building, had not been hung conventionally. Instead of being placed vertically with their bottoms thigh-high from the floor, they had been hung horizontally, spaced equally in the wall, the tops of their sashes only a few inches below the room's ceiling.

"Sounds to me like it might be somebody trying to get a look inside," he suggested. "Working around the wall looking for a window he can reach."

"My thought exactly," the editor nodded. "I had those windows set high so a burgular would need a ladder to reach them, and to keep every son of a bitch and his brother going by from staring in, so my compositors and pressmen—when I can afford to hire some—wouldn't waste their time looking out instead of tending to their jobs."

"I'll take a look-see," Longarm said, standing up. "I'll just carry this chair along and stand up in on it to look out. If it's the man I hope it is, I need to take him alive, but if he throws down on me, I'd have to shoot back."

170

Carrying the chair, Longarm started for the window at the back of the room, where Rudolph had indicated that he'd heard the last noises. Halfway to the wall, he realized that if someone was prowling along the wall the prowler would have covered some ground during his own conversation with the editor.

Unsure of the speed with which a man outside might be moving, Longarm changed his course and went to the corner nearest the blank front wall of the building. Letting the chair legs down slowly and silently, Longarm stepped up into the seat.

He was just standing up, his head still below the windowsill, when a sound of wood scraping wood rasped through the wall followed by a softer, undentifiable scraping. Longarm stood up quickly. His eyes reached the glass of the windowpane just as a man's head rose on the outside and a pair of eyes with obsidian-black pupils set in a swarthy face stared coldly into Longarm's blue eyes. The man gripped the blade of a long knife between his clenched teeth.

For a split second the two pairs of eyes locked. Then the man outside brought up his hand with a pistol in it. Longarm had started his draw while the outsider was still lifting his weapon. Bringing his Colt around with a sweeping blow, Longarm smashed its barrel through the windowpane. While the sounds of breaking glass still hung in the air, he slashed down with the heavy Colt and knocked the other man's weapon from his hand.

With a speed of a striking rattler the man grabbed for the knife-hilt. The sweeping force of Longarm's blow had carried his Colt beyond the intruder's head, but Longarm moved with dazzling speed.

At the apex of his swing he reversed the direction of his arm and with a backswing brought the Colt down on the side of his opponent's face. The obsidian eyes went blank and disappeared from Longarm's field of vision as the intruder toppled to one side and fell to the ground, where he landed with a thud.

Longarm gathered his legs with a quick downward bend and dove head-first through the window.

171

Kicking and twisting as he plummeted down, Longarm landed on his feet. The other man was beginning to stir. Stepping to his side, Longarm kicked the knife out of reach, pulled his handcuffs from his belt, and snapped them on the man's wrists. Just as he was raising up, Rudolph came rushing around the front corner of the building.

"By God," he said, "you got the Kiowa Kid!"

"Just in time to keep him from maybe getting you and me both," Longarm replied.

"How the devil did he get up high enough to look in that window?" Rudolph frowned. "He looked like he was just standing there with nothing under him but thin air."

"Oh, he had something to stand on," Longarm replied. He pointed to a wide, thick board lying on the ground beside the building. "You oughta not leave things like that lying around. He just leaned that board up under the window and shinnied up."

"Hell!" Rudolph exploded. "That's the board I put across the gutter for a bridge when it's raining!" He shook his head. "Well, I learned a lesson about being careful, and you learned a lesson, too, I guess."

"Now what kind of lesson would that be?"

"Never underestimate the power of the press," Rudolph replied. "As I see it, it brought you the Kiowa Kid when you were just about ready to give up."

"Hold on, now," Longarm cautioned. "I don't give up all that easy. Even if I'd've left here, I'd've looked someplace else that was a likely spot for him to hole up."

"Just the same, the Kiowa Kid's your prisoner now."

"I got a prisoner here, all right, except I ain't sure who in hell he is," Longarm replied.

"Now, hold on!" Rudolph protested. "You said—"

Longarm broke in, "Now don't go getting riled up. I got a real strong hunch he's the man I'm after. But whoever he is, he's just passing as the Kiowa Kid."

"I don't follow you," Rudolph frowned. "You said yourself that you were looking—"

"Sure," Longarm interrupted. "This fellow ain't the only one travelling under that name, but there ain't much chance

172

he was just prowling along your wall here without having no reason to. Anyhow, I'm right sure he's the one I come here to bring back. It'll all be unravelled when I get him back to Denver."

By now the man on the ground was stirring. Longarm leaned over him and lifted him by the handcuff links. On his feet, the prisoner swayed for a moment, his eyes closed. Then he fixed their black depths on Longarm.

"You lie, Long! I am Kiowa Kid!"

"I'm glad you admit it," Longarm replied. He turned back to Rudolph and said, "I got to thank you, Rudy, for all your help. I'd stick around to have a few drinks with you and all the rest of you folks, like Jim McMasters, that give me a hand here in Tascosa. But it's getting on for noon, and it's a long ride to get to a railroad that'll take me into Denver." He jerked his prisoner by the handcuff chain and said, "Come on, whoever you are. We got a sight of travelling to do, and we might as well get started."

Chapter 20

"All right, Billy," Longarm told Vail. "I got your Kiowa Kid safe and sound in a holdover cell down at the city jail."

"It took you long enough," Vail said. "What'd you do, stop along the way to play a game of checkers? Or did you run across a girl somewhere?"

"I just did the best I could with what I had to work with," Longarm replied calmly. "First off, I had to traipse over half of the Indian Nation before old Quanah Parker tipped me to look for him in the Texas Panhandle. Then it took me a while to nab him, and even when I had the cuffs on him I had to go across some mighty rough country after I left Tascosa to where I could board a train to get back here to Denver."

"Well, I'd just about given up on you. The least you could have done was to send me a wire when you arrested him."

"I did, Billy," Longarm protested. "But in case you've forgot where Tascosa is, it's a four-day trip from there to

174

the closest telegraph office, which is way up in the northeast corner of the Texas Panhandle."

"You don't have to remind me where anyplace in Texas is, damn it!" Vail said impatiently. "I was a Texas Ranger long enough to learn about the geography down there."

Longarm was determined to have his say. "What's more," he told Vail, "till I got off in Trinidad to change trains for Denver, I wasn't sure whether I was supposed to bring in the Kiowa Kid I'd captured or take him south and hand him over to the Texas Rangers in Austin."

For a moment Vail sat silent, then he nodded. "All right. I guess you did the best you could, at that."

"It's real nice of you to admit it, Billy," Longarm told his chief. "Even if it was a long time before you could get yourself around to it. But that's neither here nor there. What's Will Travers done since I left Austin?"

"I had a wire from him the day before yesterday," Vail said. "And he finally got that judge down on the Rio Grande to release him. "They caught the Kiowa Kid that escaped from jail down there. Will sent the wire from Laredo, and he ought to be back in Austin by now."

"So we got one Kiowa Kid here in Denver, and Will and his outfit's got another one down in Texas," Longarm frowned. "How do we go about getting 'em sorted out and figure which one's which?"

"Damned if I know," Vail admitted. "It's a mixed-up mess of jurisdiction, for sure. And I'm not going to ask any of our government attorneys to give me advice. If I get them involved in it, we'll be paying the Denver city jail to keep him for the next ten years before they come up with an answer."

"I figure that means you're going to settle it up private between us and the Rangers, then?"

Vail nodded. "That's what I'm thinking about now. When I wired Will I suggested that we get together somewhere about halfway between Denver and Austin and see which one of us gets which Kiowa Kid."

"Meaning we'll tote the Kiowa Kid we've got to whatever

town you and Will picks out, and they'll bring theirs?"

"Something like that," Vail agreed. "We'll sit down and compare notes. Right now, we know what the one you brought in can be tried for, and by the time we meet with Will he'll have found out what the one he's holding can be charged with."

"Well, I sure hope you and Will can get this mess settled so both of 'em are tried for a hanging crime. I'm getting damn tired of running down Kiowa Kids, Billy."

"I feel about the same way you do," Vail admitted. "That's why I want you to spend every minute of your time questioning that one we've got until Will and I set up a meeting."

"Ain't I even going to have a day off so I can get some laundry done and spend a night in my own bed?"

"Well, I don't expect you to sleep at the jail," Vail replied. "But until I change your assignment, all I expect you to do is question that prisoner you brought in. That's an order. So get back over to the jail and get started. I'll be over myself just as soon as I hear from Will Travers."

"We'll be taking the night train south," Vail announced when he arrived at the Denver city jail in the late afternoon. "Will Travers wants to bring his Kiowa Kid up to Chilicothe and meet us there. It's about as far from Austin as Denver is, so I suppose he's being fair about it. I just got his wire an hour or so ago, and the clerk's getting our travel papers up now."

"I sure ain't got a lot from this little bastard I been questioning," Longarm told him, jerking a thumb over his shoulder at the Kiowa Kid in the cell behind him.

Vail looked past Longarm at the man humped down on the bunk in the jail cell. He said, "He doesn't even look like he's got any Kiowa blood in him, except for his eyes."

"Well, he ain't got much," Longarm replied. "But when I put together what I pried outa him today and what he let fall on the way up here from Tascosa, I guess I made a start."

"You want to pass it on to me now, or wait until we're on the train tonight?"

176

"I don't know about you, Billy, but I aim to be sleeping tonight. Anyhow, it won't take long for you to listen to what I found out."

"Go ahead, then," Vail nodded.

"Well, for one thing, he ain't even a full-blood Kiowa. He don't even have his own Kiowa name! His mother was Kiowa–Apache, not pure Kiowa, and his old man was Mexican. All I could pry outa him about why he was calling himself the Kiowa Kid was that he heard the name someplace and liked the way it sounded."

"I guess he's got a real name, hasn't he?"

Longarm snorted. "Wilbur Smith! Damned if I wouldn't change my name too, if I was saddled with a namby-pamby one like that!"

"Well, name or no name, we'll haul him down to Chilicothe and let Will Travers question him."

"Hell's bells, Billy, if you ain't forget my report so soon, I got this Wilbur Smith Kiowa Kid dead to rights on them two killings I told you about in Texas. Ain't that all them Rangers need?"

"I'm not making any remarks about that," Vail replied a bit stiffly. "But it's Will's idea that the man the Rangers caught might've been into a couple of mail robberies. If you remember, we've still got our files open on two post-office holdups, and a postal clerk was killed in each of them."

"We oughta be about even, then," Longarm frowned. "It don't seem like to me this trip's really necessary, Billy."

"Necessary or not, we're leaving tonight and taking this prisoner with us. We'll have to pay the city for holding him today, so let the jail feed him his supper before you pick him up. I'll meet you at the depot at seven."

When Longarm and Vail, their handcuffed prisoner between them, got off the train at the Chilicothe depot late in the afternoon, Will Travers was not the only one waiting to welcome them. Linc Sawyer, the town marshal, and his daughter Christina were standing beside the Ranger on the station platform.

"You know, I wasn't expecting to see you again so soon," Longarm told Tina.

"Well, it's nice to see you again, Marshal Long," she said in a cool, distant voice.

When the handshakes and introductions had been completed, Vail, Travers, and Sawyer gathered around the Kiowa Kid, talking, and Longarm stepped aside. Tina joined him at once.

"I hope you really are glad to see me," she said, her voice just above whisper. "I didn't wait for Daddy to invite me when he said he was coming to the station to meet you. I just acted like it was natural for him to want me to be along."

"Now, I couldn't just grab you up and kiss you, could I?" Longarm asked. "You oughta know how glad I am."

"Well, I'm certainly glad I didn't go to a lot of trouble for nothing," Tina said. "Because since that time we had in the brakes, I've been wishing for more of the same."

"I don't see how we're going to be able to—"

"I do," she interrupted. "But I don't have time now to explain. The only thing you have to do is to get sleepy right after supper and go to your room in the hotel."

"But I ain't even got a room yet," Longarm told her.

"Yes, you have," she replied. "When Daddy got Captain Travers's wire from Austin, telling him you and Marshal Vail were going to meet him here, he had me arrange for your rooms and for dinner for all of you, and he's going to eat with you. Now, don't worry about anything else; just do what I told you to."

Before Longarm could ask Tina any questions, Vail called to him, "We'll want you with us, Long. Will's anxious to get started questioning this fellow, and Sawyer's going to join us. You know he's got an interest in the case, since the Kiowa Kid killed his night marshal here."

When Longarm rejoined the others, Vail went on, "We're going to put our man in Marshal Sawyer's jail. Will's prisoner's already there. Then we'll do our talking in Sawyer's office."

"Suits me," Longarm nodded.

As they walked slowly along, Travers said to Vail, "Billy, ever since I got your wire that Longarm had brought in your Kiowa Kid I been wondering if you found out his real name."

"Sure," Vail smiled. "Turned out to be Wilbur Smith."

When the chuckles died down, the Ranger said, "The one my boys brought gave us his name as Johnny Brown."

"I'll bet we find out that neither one of them ever even saw the real Kiowa Kid," Sawyer said.

"You're likely right," Longarm nodded.

In Marshal Sawyer's office, Sawyer locked the Kiowa Kid captured by Longarm into a cell adjoining the one occupied by the Kiowa Kid brought to Chilicothe by Will Travers.

"Damned if those two don't look enough alike to be kin," Sawyer commented as he joined the others. "I can tell 'em apart, but I got a real good personal reason for remembering the son of a bitch Marshal Vail and Longarm brought with 'em. He's the one that murdered my night man and give me this." He held up his right arm, which he still carried in a sling.

"Of course, if Will's men had brought that one in, him killing your night man would be a hanging crime in Texas," Vail commented.

"Now, hold on, Billy!" Travers broke in. "That Kiowa Kid my boys brought in has confessed to killing a postmaster over in Arizona Territory. That's a hanging job, too!"

"Now you hold on, this time," Vail told the Ranger. "You can't hang a man in Texas for a murder he committed in Arizona Territory. That's federal jurisdiction! Why, any jackleg lawyer he hired would get him off just on a damn technicality!"

"You might be right, Marshal Vail," Sawyer broke in. "If that's the case, I'd say you and Captain Travers had just better agree your bet's off."

When Vail and Travers looked at one another, both frowning, Longarm broke in, "Billy, you didn't say anything about you and Will having a bet on this case. I'd like to know what it is."

Travers questioned Vail with his eyes. After hesitating for a moment, the federal man nodded. "Go on, Will. Since we were betting on Longarm, I guess he's got a right to know."

"It was when I stopped in to talk to Billy," the Ranger told Longarm. "We were having a friendly drink and both of us got to doing a little bragging. I don't need to go on about what we said, but Billy and me bet a case of good drinking liquor on whether you or my boys would be the first to bring in the man my outfit was after."

"We didn't know then about there being two Kiowa Kids on the loose," Vail broke in. "And when we found out, we just let the bet stand."

"I guess the only thing we can do is call the bet off, the way things have turned out," Travers went on. "There's not any way to settle it, now that you and my Rangers have brought in one apiece."

"Looks like Captain Travers is right," Linc Sawyer agreed. "It's a dead heat with no winner."

"I wouldn't say that, now," Longarm said quickly. He turned to face Vail and asked, "Did I hear right that you and Will was betting on me bringing back the man the Rangers wanted?"

"That was our bet," Vail nodded. "If you brought the Kiowa Kid in before Will's Rangers did, he was stuck for a case of good drinking whiskey. But it's a dead heat, so the bet's off."

"I don't see how you figure that," Longarm said slowly. "I brought in my man, and he's the one the Rangers want."

"But we've got two Kiowa Kids," Travers protested. "You brought in one, my boys brought in another one, and we want both of them, so it's a standoff."

Longarm shook his head. "I don't figure it that way. You got a man you can't be sure of getting a hanging verdict on, but the Kiowa Kid I got killed a town marshal right here in Chilicothe, and with Marshal Sawyer for a star witness, he's bound to swing."

"But he's your prisoner!" Travers protested.

"Well, you got a man that killed a U. S. postmaster over

in Arizona Territory, which is federal jurisdiction," Longarm went on. "Now, I'd say was you and Billy to swap Kiowa Kids, you'd have the man you want, and Billy'd have the one he wants."

"Sounds to me like Longarm's talking sense," Linc Sawyer put in. "Now, I'll throw in on that scheme of his. If anybody starts claiming you made a mistake, I'll stand up and say I just got confused and handed you the wrong man."

"Well, the case against the Kiowa Kid we've got is pretty open and shut," Travers said thoughtfully.

"Is taking him back worth the price of a case of whiskey, Will?" Vail asked. "Because my bet was that Longarm would bring back your man, and that makes me winner."

"It's worth the price," Travers nodded. "And since I went to Laredo and brought my prisoner back to Austin, my men won't know the difference."

"Then I'm willing to swap if you are," Vail said.

Before Travers could answer, Longarm spoke. Turning to face Vail, he said. "I only got one thing to say. Seeing as how it was my idea, Billy, I'd expect you to tell Will you want a case of Tom Moore, and I'd take it kindly if you'd split it with me."

"Done!" Vail agreed. "And now that we've all got what we want, let's go get some supper."

They started swapping yarns midway through the meal and continued through dessert, and as they stood up after finishing their coffee Linc said, "Seeing as none of us got to get up early tomorrow, I say we might as well make a night of it. Now, Chilicothe ain't as big as Denver or even Austin, but we got some right nice saloons here. My favorite one's right around the corner. Let's go wet our whistles."

"It ain't that I don't like the company," Longarm said. "But Billy'll tell you that I've spent damn near a month without sleeping in a bed, and I figure I'm overdue for some shuteye."

"Well, if you feel like you got to go to bed, there's a room for you just down the street," Sawyer told him. "All you got to do is walk in and tell the night man to give you the key."

"Thanks, Linc," Longarm nodded. "And, meaning no insult to good company, that's just what I aim to do."

"Oh, I'm getting there fast, Longarm!" Tina gasped. Her hips were moving faster and faster in response to Longarm's steady downard thrusts.

"You want me stop a while?" Longarm asked her. "Because I ain't going to be ready for a long time."

"I don't care how long it takes you! Just don't slow down. I'm loving every minute of it."

Longarm kept up his long, deep drives while Tina's wiry body writhed beneath him. She was trembling, and her long sighs were turning into small, explosive gusts as Longarm increased the tempo of his lunges.

"I can't wait for you any longer!" she panted. "Now, right now, Longarm!"

As her body shook with the beginning of her orgasm, Longarm maintained his tempo until Tina's ecstatic scream broke the night air. Her shudder peaked and then subsided into contented sighs. She lay quivering while Longarm held himself pressed close against her. When her last wave subsided and died away he let Tina lie motionless for a while before he resumed his slow steady thrusting, and even then she did not repond at once. When he continued plunging without varying the timing of his drives, she came suddenly to life. She bounced her buttocks off the bed as she raised them to meet Longarm's increasing speed, and locked her ankles to lift herself closer and take him in deeper.

Longarm was reaching his own peak now. He pounded faster, holding himself in check, waiting for Tina to catch up. When her cries began rising once more, Longarm speeded his thrusts.

She screamed into a final explosion, and he thrust for the last time and began to jet. Tina's cry of release rang out and faded and they lay trembling, still locked together, until her cries faded to long, throaty, gasping breaths and both of them lay still.

"Even though that was our best yet, I hope you won't send me home right away," Tina sighed at last.

"Now, you know I wouldn't do that," Longarm said. "And you don't need to worry about how late it gets, because like I told you, your daddy's not likely to be home till daybreak."

"Good," Tina sighed. "Now hold me tight a little while. It won't be long before I'll be ready to start again."

Watch for

**LONGARM AND THE RANCHER'S
SHOWDOWN**

eighty-eighth novel in the bold
LONGARM series from Jove

coming in April!